THE SUSPECT

"We're looking for a stranger, six foot tall, wearing newish Dunlop Wellington boots size 10½, leather gloves and an old blue overcoat stained with blood. A man who travels on foot, who was in the area of North Fields between 11:10 and 11:45 on the night of the murder, who left in the direction of Okeford, taking with him one and a half feet of coaxial cable, a string of green beads and an imitation diamond clip. We're looking for a maniac, a man who kills for pleasure or the price of a meal . . . who can fly fifty feet through the air."

LE CARRÉ
A MURDER OF QUALITY

CALL FOR THE DEAD
THE HONOURABLE SCHOOLBOY
THE LOOKING GLASS WAR
A MURDER OF QUALITY
THE NAIVE AND SENTIMENTAL LOVER
SMILEY'S PEOPLE
THE SPY WHO CAME IN FROM THE COLD
TINKER, TAILOR, SOLDIER, SPY

A MURDER
OF
QUALITY

John le Carré

BANTAM BOOKS
TORONTO · NEW YORK · LONDON · SYDNEY

A MURDER OF QUALITY

*A Bantam Book / published by arrangement with
Walker & Company*

PRINTING HISTORY

Walker & Company edition published August 1968

*Bantam edition / January 1980
7 printings through December 1988*

ISBN 0-553-23902-3

PRINTED IN THE UNITED STATES OF AMERICA

H   16 15 14 13 12 11 10 9 8 7

A MURDER
OF
QUALITY

I

Black Candles

The greatness of Carne School has been ascribed by common consent to Edward VI, whose educational zeal is ascribed by history to the Duke of Somerset. But Carne prefers the respectability of the monarch to the questionable politics of his adviser, drawing strength from the conviction that Great Schools, like Tudor Kings, were ordained in Heaven.

And indeed its greatness is little short of miraculous. Founded by obscure monks, endowed by a sickly boy king, and dragged from oblivion by a Victorian bully, Carne had straightened its collar, scrubbed its rustic hands and face and presented itself shining to the courts of the twentieth century. And in the twinkling of an eye, the Dorset bumpkin was London's darling: Dick Whittington had arrived. Carne had parchments in Latin, seals in wax and Lammas Land behind the Abbey. Carne had property, cloisters and woodworm, a whipping block and a line in the Doomsday Book—then what more did it need to instruct the sons of the rich?

And they came; each Half they came (for terms are not elegant things), so that throughout a whole afternoon the trains would unload sad groups of black-coated boys on to the station platform. They came in great cars that shone with mournful purity. They came

1

to bury poor King Edward, trundling handcarts over the cobbled streets or carrying tuck boxes like little coffins. Some wore gowns, and when they walked they looked like crows, or black angels come for the burying. Some followed singly like undertakers' mutes, and you could hear the clip of their boots as they went. They were always in mourning at Carne; the small boys because they must stay and the big boys because they must leave, the masters because mourning was respectable and the wives because respectability was underpaid; and now, as the Lent Half (as the Easter term was called) drew to its end, the cloud of gloom was as firmly settled as ever over the grey towers of Carne.

Gloom and the cold. The cold was crisp and sharp as flint. It cut the faces of the boys as they moved slowly from the deserted playing fields after the school match. It pierced their black topcoats and turned their stiff, pointed collars into icy rings round their necks. Frozen, they plodded from the field to the long walled road which led to the main tuck shop and the town, the line gradually dwindling into groups, and the groups into pairs. Two boys who looked even colder than the rest crossed the road and made their way along a narrow path which led towards a distant but less populated tuck shop.

"I think I shall die if ever I have to watch one of those beastly rugger games again. The noise is fantastic," said one. He was tall with fair hair, and his name was Caley.

"People only shout because the dons are watching from the pavilion," the other rejoined; "that's why each house has to stand together. So that the house dons can swank about how loud their houses shout."

"What about Rode?" asked Caley. "Why does he stand with us and make us shout, then? He's not a house don, just a bloody usher."

"He's sucking up to house dons all the time. You can see him in the quad between lessons buzzing round the big men. All the junior masters do." Caley's companion was a cynical red-haired boy called Perkins, Captain of Fielding's house.

"I've been to tea with Rode," said Caley.

"Rode's hell. He wears brown boots. What was tea like?"

"Bleak. Funny how tea gives them away. Mrs. Rode's quite decent, though—homely in a plebby sort of way: doilies and china birds. Food's good: Women's Institute, but good."

"Rode's doing Corps next Half. That'll put the lid on it. He's so *keen,* bouncing about all the time. You can tell he's not a gentleman. You know where he went to school?"

"No."

"Branxome Grammar. Fielding told my Mama, when she came over from Singapore last Half."

"God. Where's Branxome?"

"On the coast. Near Bournemouth. I haven't been to tea with anyone except Fielding." Perkins added after a slight pause, "You get roast chestnuts and crumpets. You're never allowed to thank him, you know. He says emotionalism is only for the lower classes. That's typical of Fielding. He's not like a don at all. I think boys bore him. The whole house goes to tea with him once a half, he has us in turn, four at a time, and that's about the only time he talks to most men."

They walked on in silence for a while until Perkins said:

"Fielding's giving another dinner party tonight."

"He's pushing the boat out these days," Caley replied, with disapproval. "Suppose the food in your house is worse than ever?"

"It's his last Half before he retires. He's entertaining every don and all the wives separately by the end of the Half. Black candles every evening. For mourning. Hells extravagant."

"Yes. I suppose it's a sort of gesture."

"My Pater says he's a queer."

They crossed the road and disappeared into the tuck shop, where they continued to discuss the weighty affairs of Mr. Terence Fielding, until Perkins drew their meeting reluctantly to a close. Being a poor hand at science, he was unfortunately obliged to take extra tuition in the subject.

The dinner party to which Perkins had alluded that afternoon was now drawing to a close. Mr. Terence Fielding, senior housemaster of Carne, gave himself some more port and pushed the decanter wearily to his left. It was his port, the best he had. There was enough of the best to last the Half—and after that, be damned. He felt a little tired after watching the match, and a little drunk, and a little bored with Shane Hecht and her husband. Shane was so hideous. Massive and enveloping, like a faded Valkyrie. All that black hair. He should have asked someone else. The Snows for instance, but he was too clever. Or Felix D'Arcy, but D'Arcy interrupted. Ah well, a little later he would annoy Charles Hecht, and Hecht would get in a pet and leave early.

Hecht was fidgeting, wanting to light his pipe, but Fielding damn well wouldn't have it. Hecht could have a cigar if he wanted to smoke. But his pipe could stay in his dinner-jacket pocket, where it belonged, or didn't belong, and his athletic profile could remain unadorned.

"Cigar, Hecht?"

"No thanks, Fielding. I say, do you mind if I . . ."

"I can recommend the cigars. Young Havelake sent them from Havana. His father's ambassador there, you know."

"Yes, dear," said Shane tolerantly; "Vivian Havelake was in Charles' troop when Charles was commandant of the Cadets."

"Good boy, Havelake," Hecht observed, and pressed his lips together to show he was a strict judge.

"It's amusing how things have changed." Shane Hecht said this rapidly with a rather wooden smile, as if it weren't really amusing. "Such a grey world we live in, now.

"I remember before the war when Charles inspected the Corps on a white horse. We don't do that kind of thing now, do we? I've got nothing against Mr. Iredale as commandant, nothing at all. What *was* his regiment, Terence, do you know? I'm sure he does it very nicely, whatever they do now in the Corps—he gets on so well with the boys, doesn't he? His wife's such a nice person. . . . I wonder why they can never keep their servants. I hear Mr. Rode will be helping out with the Corps next Half."

"Poor little Rode," said Fielding slowly; "running about like a puppy, trying to earn his biscuits. He tries so hard; have you seen him cheering at school matches? He'd never seen a game of rugger before he came here, you know. They don't play rugger at grammar schools—it's all soccer. Do you remember when he first came, Charles? It was fascinating. He lay very low at first, drinking us in: the games, the vocabulary, the manners. Then, one day it was as if he had been given the power of speech, and he spoke in our language. It was amazing, like plastic surgery. It was Felix D'Arcy's work of course—I've never seen anything quite like it before."

"Dear Mrs. Rode," said Shane Hecht in that voice of abstract vagueness which she reserved for her most venomous pronouncements: "So sweet . . . and such simple taste, don't you think? I mean, whoever would have dreamed of putting those china ducks on the wall? Big ones at the front and little ones at the back. Charming, don't you think? Like one of those teashops. I wonder where she bought them. I must ask her. I'm told her father lives near Bournemouth. It must be so lonely for him, don't you think? Such a vulgar place; no one to talk to."

Fielding sat back and surveyed his own table. The silver was good. The best in Carne, he had heard it said, and he was inclined to agree. This Half he had nothing but black candles. It was the sort of thing people remembered when you'd gone: "Dear old Terence— marvellous host. He dined every member of the staff during his last Half, you know, wives too. Black candles, rather touching. It broke his heart giving up his house." But he must annoy Charles Hecht. Shane would like that. Shane would egg him on because she hated

Charles, because within her great ugly body she was as cunning as a snake.

Fielding looked at Hecht and then at Hecht's wife, and she smiled back at him, the slow rotten smile of a whore. For a moment Fielding thought of Hecht pasturing in that thick body: it was a scene redolent of Lautrec . . . yes, that was it! Charles pompous and tophatted, seated stiffly upon the plush coverlet; she massive, pendulous and bored. The image pleased him: so perverse to consign that fool Hecht from the Spartan cleanliness of Carne to the brothels of nineteenth-century Paris. . . .

Fielding began talking, pontificating rather, with an air of friendly objectivity which he knew Hecht would resent.

"When I look back on my thirty years at Carne, I realise I have achieved rather less than a roadsweeper." They were watching him now—"I used to regard a roadsweeper as a person inferior to myself. Now, I rather doubt it. Something is dirty, he makes it clean, and the state of the world is advanced. But I—what have *I* done. Entrenched a ruling class which is distinguished by neither talent, culture nor wit; kept alive for one more generation the distinctions of a dead age."

Charles Hecht, who had never perfected the art of not listening to Fielding, grew red and fussed at the other end of the table.

"Don't we teach them, Fielding? What about our successes, our scholarships?"

"I have never taught a boy in my life, Charles. Usually the boy wasn't clever enough; occasionally, I wasn't. In most boys, you see, perception dies with puberty. In a few it persists, though where we find it we take good care at Carne to kill it. If it survives our efforts the boy wins a scholarship. . . . Bear with me, Shane; it's my last Half."

"Last Half or not, you're talking through your hat, Fielding," said Hecht, angrily.

"That is traditional at Carne. These successes, as you call them, are the failures, the rare boys who have not learned the lessons of Carne. They have ignored the cult of mediocrity. We can do nothing for them. But for the rest, for the puzzled little clerics and the blind little soldiers, for them the truth of Carne is written on the wall, and they hate us."

Hecht laughed rather heavily.

"Why do so many come back, then, if they hate us so much? Why do they remember us and come and see us?"

"Because we, dear Charles, are the writing on the wall! The one lesson of Carne they never forget. They come back to read *us*, don't you see? It was from us they learnt the secret of life: that we grow old without growing wise. They realised that nothing happened when we grew up: no blinding light on the road to Damascus, no sudden feeling of maturity." Fielding put his head back and gazed at the clumsy Victorian moulding on the ceiling, and the halo of dirt round the light rose.

"We just got a little older. We made the same jokes, thought the same thoughts, wanted the same things. Year in, year out, Hecht, we were the same people, not wiser, not better; we haven't had an original thought between us for the last fifty years of our lives. They saw what a trick it all was, Carne and us; our academic dress, our schoolroom jokes, our wise little offerings of guidance. And that's why they come back year after year of their puzzled, barren lives to gaze fascinated at you and me, Hecht, like children at a grave, searching for the secret of life and death. Oh, yes, they have learned *that* from us."

Hecht looked at Fielding in silence for a moment.

"Decanter, Hecht?" said Fielding, in a slightly conciliatory way, but Hecht's eyes were still upon him.

"If that's a joke . . ." he began, and his wife observed with satisfaction that he was very angry indeed.

"I wish I knew, Charles," Fielding replied with apparent earnestness. "I really wish I knew. I used to think it was clever to confuse comedy with tragedy. Now I wish I could distinguish them." He rather liked that.

They had coffee in the drawing-room, where Fielding resorted to gossip, but Hecht was not to be drawn. Fielding rather wished he had let him light his pipe. Then he recalled his vision of the Hechts in Paris, and it restored him. He had been rather good this evening. There were moments when he convinced himself.

While Shane fetched her coat, the two men stood together in the hall, but neither spoke. Shane returned, an ermine stole, yellow with age, draped over her great white shoulders. She inclined her head to the right, smiled and held out her hand to Fielding, the fingers down.

"Terence, darling," she said, as Fielding kissed her fat knuckles; "so kind. And in your last Half. You must dine with us before you go. So sad. So few of us left." She smiled again, half closing her eyes to indicate emotional disturbance, then followed her husband into the street. It was still bitterly cold and snow was in the air.

Fielding closed and carefully bolted the door behind them—perhaps a fraction earlier than courtesy required—and returned to the dining room. Hecht's port glass was still about half full. Fielding picked it up and carefully poured the contents back into the decanter. He hoped Hecht wasn't too upset; he hated people to dislike him. He snuffed the black candles and damped their wicks between his forefinger and thumb. Switching on the light, he took from the sideboard a sixpenny notebook, and opened it. It contained his list of dining guests for the remainder of the Half. With his fountain pen he placed a neat tick against the name Hecht. They were done. On Wednesday he would have the Rodes. The husband was quite good value, but she, of course, was hell. . . . It was not always the way with married couples. The wives as a rule were so much more sympathetic.

He opened the sideboard and took from it a bottle of brandy and a tumbler. Holding them both in the same hand, he shuffled wearily back to the drawing room, resting his other hand on the wall as he went. God! He felt old, suddenly; that thin line of pain across the chest, that heaviness in the legs and feet. Such an effort being with people—on stage all the time. He hated to be alone, but people bored him. Being alone was like being tired, but unable to sleep. Some German poet had said that; he'd quoted it once, "You may sleep but I must dance." Something like that.

"That's how I am," thought Fielding. "That's how Carne is, too; an old satyr dancing to the music." The music grew faster and their bodies older, but they must dance on—there were young men waiting in the wings. It had been funny once dancing the old dances in a new world. He poured himself some more brandy. He'd be pleased to leave in a way, even though he'd have to go on teaching somewhere else.

But it had its beauty, Carne. . . . The Abbey Close in spring . . . the flamingo figures of boys waiting for the ritual of worship . . . the ebb and flow of children, like the seasons of the year, and the old men dying among them. He wished he could paint; he would paint the pageant of Carne in the fallow browns of autumn. . . . What a shame, thought Fielding, that a mind so perceptive of beauty had no talent for creation.

He looked at his watch. Quarter to twelve. Nearly time to go out . . . to dance, and not to sleep.

II

The Thursday Feeling

It was Thursday evening and the *Christian Voice* had just been put to bed. This was scarcely an historic event in Fleet Street. The pimply boy from Despatch who took away the ragged pile of page-proofs showed no more ceremony than was strictly demanded by the eventual prospect of his Christmas bonus. And even in this respect he had learned that the secular journals of Unipress were more provident of material charity than the *Christian Voice*; charity being in strict relationship to circulation.

Miss Brimley, the journal's editor, adjusted the air cushion beneath her and lit a cigarette. Her secretary and sub-editor—the appointment carried both responsibilities—yawned, dropped the aspirin bottle into her handbag, combed out her ginger hair and bade Miss Brimley good night, leaving behind her as usual the smell of strongly scented powder and an empty paper-tissue box. Miss Brimley listened contentedly to the clipping echo of her footsteps as it faded down the corridor. It pleased her to be alone at last, tasting the anticlimax. She never failed to wonder at herself, how every Thursday morning brought the same slight uneasiness as she entered the vast Unipress building and stood a little absurdly on one escalator after the other, like a drab parcel on a luxury liner. Heaven knows, she had run the

Voice for fourteen years, and there were those who said
its layout was the best thing Unipress did. Yet the
Thursday feeling never left her, the wakeful anxiety that
one day, perhaps today, they wouldn't be ready when
the despatch boy came. She often wondered what would
happen then. She had heard of failures elsewhere in that
vast combine, of features disapproved and staff re-
buked. It was a mystery to her why they kept the *Voice*
at all, with its expensive room on the seventh floor and
a circulation which, if Miss Brimley knew anything,
hardly paid for the paper-clips.

The *Voice* had been founded at the turn of the
century by old Lord Landsbury, together with a Nonconformist daily newspaper and the *Temperance Gazette*. But the *Gazette* and the daily were long since
dead, and Landsbury's son had woken one morning not
long ago to find his whole business and every man and
woman of it, every stick of furniture, ink, paper-clips
and galley-pins, bought by the hidden gold of Unipress.

That was three years ago and every day she had
waited for her dismissal. But it never came; no direc-
tive, no question, no word. And so, being a sensible
woman, she continued exactly as before and ceased to
wonder.

And she was glad. It was easy to sneer at the
Voice. Every week it offered humbly and without fan-
fares evidence of the Lord's intervention in the world's
affairs, retold in simple and somewhat unscientific
terms the early history of the Jews, and provided over a
fictitious signature motherly advice to whomever should
write and ask for it. The *Voice* scarcely concerned itself
with the fifty-odd millions of the population who had
never heard of it. It was a family affair, and rather than
abuse those who were not members, it did its best for
those who were. For them it was kind, optimistic, and
informative. If a million children were dying of the
plague in India, you may be sure that the weekly editorial described the miraculous escape from fire of a
Methodist family in Kent. The *Voice* did not advise
you how to disguise the encroaching wrinkles round
your eyes, or control your spreading figure; did not dis-

may you, if you were old, by its own eternal youth. It
was itself middle-aged and middle class, counselled cau-
tion to girls and charity to all. Nonconformity is the
most conservative of habits and families which took the
Voice in 1903 continued to take it in 1960.

Miss Brimley was not quite the image of her journal. The fortunes of war and the caprice of Intelligence
work had thrown her into partnership with the younger
Lord Landsbury, and for the six years of war they had
worked together efficiently and inconspicuously in an
unnamed building in Knightsbridge. The fortunes of
peace rendered both unemployed, but Landsbury had
the good sense, as well as the generosity, to offer Miss
Brimley a job. The *Voice* had ceased publication during the war, and no one seemed anxious to renew it. At
first Miss Brimley had felt a little ashamed at reviving
and editing a journal which in no way expressed her
own vague deism, but quite soon, as the touching letters
came in and the circulation recovered, she developed an
affection for her job—and for her readers—which
outweighed her earlier misgivings. The *Voice* was her
life, and its readers her preoccupation. She struggled to
answer their odd, troubled questions, sought advice of
others where she could not provide it herself, and in
time, under a handful of pseudonyms, became if not
their philosopher, their guide, friend and universal aunt.

Miss Brimley put out her cigarette, absently tidied
the pins, paper-clips, scissors and paste into the top
righthand drawer of her desk, and gathered together the
afternoon mail from her in-tray which, because it was
Thursday, she had left untouched. There were several
letters addressed to Barbara Fellowship, under which
name the *Voice* had, since its foundation, answered
both privately and through its published columns the
many problems of its correspondents. They could wait
until tomorrow. She rather enjoyed the "problem post,"
but Friday morning was when she read it. She opened
the little filing cabinet at her elbow and dropped the
letters into a box file at the front of the compartment.
As she did so, one of them fell on its back and she noticed with surprise that the sealed flap was embossed

with an elegant blue dolphin. She picked the envelope out of the cabinet and looked at it curiously, turning it over several times. It was of pale grey paper, very faintly lined. Expensive—perhaps hand-made. Beneath the dolphin was a tiny scroll on which she could just discern the legend, *Regem defendere diem videre*. The postmark was Carne, Dorset. That must be the school crest. But why was Carne familiar to her? Miss Brimley was proud of her memory, which was excellent, and she was vexed when it failed her. As a last resort she opened the envelope with her faded ivory paper knife and read the letter.

> *Dear Miss Fellowship,*
> *I don't know if you are a real person but it doesn't matter, because you always give such good, kind answers. It was me who wrote last June about the pastry mix. I am not mad and I know my husband is trying to kill me. Could I please come and see you as soon as it's convenient? I'm sure you'll believe me, and understand that I am normal. Could it be as soon as possible please, I am so afraid of the long nights. I don't know who else to turn to. I could try Mr. Cardew at the Tabernacle but he wouldn't believe me and Dad's too sensible. I might as well be dead. There's something not quite right about him. At night sometimes when he thinks I'm asleep he just lies watching the darkness. I know it's wrong to think such wicked things and have fear in our hearts, but I can't help it.*
> *I hope you don't get many letters like this.*
>
> *Yours faithfully,*
> *Stella Rode (Mrs.)*
> *née Glaston.*

She sat quite still at her desk for a moment, looking at the address in handsome blue engraving at the top of the page: "North Fields, Carne School, Dorset." In that moment of shock and astonishment one phrase forced itself upon her mind. "The value of intelligence depends on its breeding." That was John Landsbury's

favourite dictum. Until you know the pedigree of the
information you cannot evaluate a report. Yes, that was
what he used to say: "We are not democratic. We close
the door on intelligence without parentage." And she
used to reply: "Yes, John, but even the best families
had to begin somewhere."

But Stella Rode *had* parentage. It all came back to
her now. She was the Glaston girl. The girl whose marriage was reported in the editorial, the girl who won the
summer competition; Samuel Glaston's daughter from
Branxome. She had a card in Miss Brimley's index.

Abruptly she stood up, the letter still in her hand,
and walked to the uncurtained window. Just in front of
her was a contemporary window-box of woven white
metal. It was odd, she reflected, how she could never
get anything to grow in that window-box. She looked
down into the street, a slight, sensible figure leaning forward a little and framed by the incandescent fog outside; fog made yellow from the stolen light of London's
streets. She could just distinguish the street lamps far
below, pale and sullen. She suddenly felt the need for
fresh air, and on an impulse quite alien to her usual
calm, she opened the window wide. The quick cold and
the angry surge of noise burst in on her, and the insidi-
ous fog followed. The sound of traffic was constant, so
that for a moment she thought it was the turning of
some great machine. Then above its steady growl she
heard the newsboys. Their cries were like the cries of
gulls against a gathering storm. She could see them
now, sentinels among the hastening shadows.

It might be true. That had always been the difficulty. Right through the war it was the same restless
search. It might be true. It was no use relating reports
to probability when there was no quantum of knowledge from which to start. She remembered the first
intelligence from France on flying bombs, wild talk of
concrete runways in the depths of a forest. You had to
resist the dramatic, you had to hold out against it. Yet it
might be true. Tomorrow, the day after, those newsboys
down there might be shouting it, and Stella Rode *née*
Glaston might be dead. And if that was so, if there was

the remotest chance that this man was plotting to kill this woman, then she, Ailsa Brimley, must do what she could to prevent it. Besides, Stella Glaston had a claim on her assistance if anyone did: both her father and her grandfather had taken the *Voice*, and when Stella married five years ago Miss Brimley had put a couple of lines about it in the editorial. The Glastons sent her a Christmas card every year. They were one of the original families to subscribe. . . .

It was cold at the window, but she remained there, still fascinated by the half hidden shadows joining and parting beneath her, and the useless street lights burning painfully among them. She began to imagine him as one of those shadows, pressing and jostling, his murderer's eyes turned to sockets of dark. And suddenly she was frightened and needed help.

But not the police, not yet. If Stella Rode had wanted that she would have gone herself. Why hadn't she? For love? For fear of looking a fool? Because instinct was not evidence? They wanted fact. But the fact of murder was death. Must they wait for that?

Who would help? She thought at once of Landsbury, but he was farming in Rhodesia. Who else had been with them in the war? Fielding and Jebedee were dead, Steed Asprey vanished. Smiley—where was he? George Smiley, the cleverest and perhaps the oddest of them all. Of course, Miss Brimley remembered now. He made that improbable marriage and went back to research at Oxford. But he hadn't stayed there. . . . The marriage had broken up. . . . What *had* he done after that?

She returned to her desk and picked up the S-Z directory. Ten minutes later she was sitting in a taxi, heading for Sloane Square. In her neatly gloved hand she held a cardboard folder containing Stella Rode's card from the index and the correspondence which had passed between them at the time of the Summer Competition. She was nearly at Piccadilly when she remembered she'd left the office window open. It didn't seem to matter much.

"With other people it's Persian cats or golf. With me it's the *Voice* and my readers. I'm a ridiculous spinster, I know, but there it is. I won't go to the police until I've tried *something*, George."

"And you thought you'd try me?"

"Yes."

She was sitting in the study of George Smiley's house in Bywater Street; the only light came from the complicated lamp on his desk, a black spider of a thing shining brightly on to the manuscript notes which covered the desk.

"So you've left the Service?" she said.

"Yes, yes, I have." He nodded his round head vigorously, as if reassuring himself that a distasteful experience was really over, and mixed Miss Brimley a whisky and soda. "I had another spell there after . . . Oxford. It's all very different in peacetime, you know," he continued.

Miss Brimley nodded.

"I can imagine it. More time to be bitchy." Smiley said nothing, just lit a cigarette and sat down opposite her.

"And the people have changed. Fielding, Steed, Jebedee. All gone." She said this in a matter-of-fact way as she took from her large sensible handbag Stella Rode's letter. "This is the letter, George."

When he had read it, he held it briefly towards the lamp, his round face caught by the light in a moment of almost comic earnestness. Watching him, Miss Brimley wondered what impression he made on those who did not know him well. She used to think of him as the most forgettable man she had ever met; short and plump, with heavy spectacles and thinning hair, he was at first sight the very prototype of an unsuccessful middle-aged bachelor in a sedentary occupation. His natural diffidence in most practical matters was reflected in his clothes, which were costly and unsuitable, for he was clay in the hands of his tailor, who robbed him.

He had put down the letter on the small marquetry table beside him, and was looking at her owlishly.

"This other letter she sent you, Brim. Where is it?"

She handed him the folder. He opened it and after a moment read aloud Stella Rode's other letter:

Dear Miss Fellowship,
I would like to submit the following suggestion for your "Kitchen Hints" competition.
Make your basic batch of cake mixture once a month. Cream equal quantities of fat and sugar and add one egg for every six ounces of the mixture. For puddings and cakes, add flour to the required quantity of basic mixture.
This will keep well for a month.
I enclose stamped addressed envelope.

Yours sincerely,
Stella Rode (née Glaston).

PS.—Incidentally, you can prevent wire wool from rusting by keeping it in a jar of soapy water. Are we allowed two suggestions? If so, please can this be my second?

"She won the competition," Miss Brimley observed, "but that's not the point. This is what I want to tell you, George. She's a Glaston, and the Glastons have been reading the *Voice* since it started. Stella's grandfather was old Rufus Glaston, a Lancashire pottery king; he and John Landsbury's father built chapels and tabernacles in practically every village in the Midlands. When Rufus died the *Voice* put out a memorial edition and old Landsbury himself wrote the obituary. Samuel Glaston took on his father's business, but had to move south because of his health. He ended up near Bournemouth, a widower with one daughter, Stella. She's the last of all that family. The whole lot are as down to earth as you could wish, Stella included, I should think. I don't think any of them is likely to be suffering from delusions of persecution."

Smiley was looking at her in astonishment.

"My dear Brim, I can't possibly take that in. How on earth do you know all this?"

Miss Brimley smiled apologetically.

"The Glastons are easy—they're almost part of the

magazine. They send us Christmas cards, and boxes of chocolates on the anniversary of our foundation. We've got about five hundred families who form what I call our Establishment. They were in on the *Voice* from the start and they've kept up ever since. They write to us, George; if they're worried they write and say so; if they're getting married, moving house, retiring from work, if they're ill, depressed, or angry, they write. Not often, Heaven knows; but enough."

"How do you remember it all?"

"I don't. I keep a card index. I always write back, you see . . . only . . ."

"Yes?"

Miss Brimley looked at him earnestly.

"This is the first time anyone has written because she's frightened."

"What do you want me to do?"

"I've only had one bright idea so far. I seem to remember Adrian Fielding had a brother who taught at Carne. . . ."

"He's a housemaster there, if he hasn't retired."

"No, he retires this Half—it was in *The Times* some weeks ago, in that little bit on the Court page where Carne always announces itself. It said: 'Carne School reassembles today for the Lent Half. Mr. T. R. Fielding will retire at the end of the Half, having completed his statutory fifteen years as a housemaster.'"

Smiley laughed.

"Really, Brim, your memory is absurd!"

"It was the mention of Fielding . . . Anyway, I thought you could ring him up. You must know him."

"Yes, yes. I know him. At least, I met him once at Magdalen High Table. But——" Smiley coloured a little.

"But what, George?"

"Well he's not quite the man his brother was, you know."

"How could he be?" Miss Brimley rejoined a little sharply. "But he can tell you something about Stella Rode. And her husband."

"I don't think I could do that on the telephone. I

think I'd rather go and see him. But what's to stop you ringing up Stella Rode?"

"Well, I can't tonight, can I? Her husband will be in. I thought I'd put a letter in the post to her tonight telling her she can come to see me any time. But," she continued, making a slight, impatient movement with her foot, "I want to do something *now*, George."

Smiley nodded and went to the telephone. He rang directory enquiries and asked for Terence Fielding's number. After a long delay he was told to ring Carne School central exchange, who would connect him with whomever he required. Miss Brimley, watching him, wished she knew a little more about George Smiley, how much of that diffidence was assumed, how vulnerable he was.

"The best," Adrian had said. "The strongest and the best."

But so many men learnt strength during the war, learnt terrible things, and put aside their knowledge with a shudder when it ended.

The number was ringing now. She heard the dialling tone and for a moment was filled with apprehension. For the first time she was afraid of making a fool of herself, afraid of becoming involved in unlikely explanations with angular, suspicious people.

"Mr. Terence Fielding, please. . . ." A pause.

"Fielding, good evening. My name is George Smiley; I knew your brother well in the war. We have in fact met. . . . Yes, yes, quite right—Magdalen, was it not, the summer before last? Look, I wonder if I might come and see you on a personal matter . . . it's a little difficult to discuss on the telephone. A friend of mine has received a rather disturbing letter from the wife of a Carne master . . . Well, I—Rode, Stella Rode; her husband . . ."

He suddenly stiffened, and Miss Brimley, her eyes fixed upon him, saw with alarm how his chubby face broke into an expression of pain and disgust. She no longer heard what he was saying. She could only watch the dreadful transformation of his face, the whitening knuckles of his hand clutching the receiver. He was looking at her now, saying something . . . it was too late. Stella Rode was dead. She had been murdered late on Wednesday night. They'd actually been dining with Fielding the night it happened.

III

The Night Of The Murder

The seven-five from Waterloo to Yeovil is not a popular train, though it provides an excellent breakfast. Smiley had no difficulty in finding a first-class compartment to himself. It was a bitterly cold day, dark and the sky heavy with snow. He sat huddled in a voluminous travelling coat of Continental origin, holding in his gloved hands a bundle of the day's papers. Because he was a precise man and did not care to be hurried, he had arrived thirty minutes before the train was due to depart. Still tired after the stresses of the previous night, when he had sat up talking with Ailsa Brimley until Heaven knew what hour, he was disinclined to read. Looking out of the window on to an almost empty station, he caught sight, to his great surprise, of Miss Brimley herself making her way along the platform, peering in at the windows, a carrier bag in her hand. He lowered the window and called to her.

"My dear Brim, what are you doing here at this dreadful hour? You should be in bed."

She sat down opposite him and began unpacking her bag and handing him its contents: thermos, sandwiches and chocolate.

"I didn't know whether there was a breakfast car," she explained; "and besides, I wanted to come and see you off. You're such a dear, George, and I wish I could

21

come with you, but Unipress would go mad if I did. The only time they notice you is when you're not there."

"Have you seen the papers?" he asked.

"Just briefly, on the way here. They seem to think it wasn't him, but some madman. . . ."

"I know, Brim. That's what Fielding said, wasn't it?" There was a moment's awkward silence.

"George, am I being an awful ass, letting you go off like this? I was so sure last night, but now I wonder . . ."

"After you left I rang Ben Sparrow of Special Branch. You remember him, don't you? He was with us in the war. I told him the whole story."

"George! At three in the morning?"

"Yes. He's ringing the Divisional Superintendent at Carne. He'll tell him about the letter, and that I'm coming down. Ben had an idea that a man named Rigby would be handling the case. Rigby and Ben were at police college together." He looked at her kindly for a moment. "Besides, I'm a man of leisure, Brim. I shall enjoy the change."

"Bless you, George," said Miss Brimley, woman enough to believe him. She got up to go, and Smiley said to her:

"Brim, if you should need any more help or anything, and can't get hold of me, there's a man called Mendel who lives in Mitcham, a retired police inspector. He's in the book. If you get hold of him and mention me, he'll do what he can for you. I've booked a room at the Sawley Arms."

Alone again, Smiley surveyed uneasily the assortment of food and drink which Miss Brimley had provided. He had promised himself the luxury of breakfast in the restaurant car. He would keep the sandwiches and coffee for later, that would be the best thing; for lunch, perhaps. And he would breakfast properly.

In the restaurant car Smiley read first the less sensational reports on the death of Stella Rode. It appeared that on Wednesday evening Mr. and Mrs. Rode had been guests at dinner of Mr. Terence Fielding, the senior housemaster at Carne and brother of the late Adrian

Fielding, the celebrated French scholar who had vanished during the war while specially employed by the War Office. They had left Mr. Fielding's house together at about ten to eleven and walked the half mile from the centre of Carne to their house, which stood alone at the edge of the famous Carne playing fields. As they reached their house Mr. Rode remembered that he had left at Mr. Fielding's house some examination papers which urgently required correction that night. (At this point Smiley remembered that he had failed to pack his dinner jacket, and that Fielding would almost certainly ask him to dine.) Rode determined to walk back to Fielding's house and collect the papers, therefore, starting back at about five past eleven. It appears that Mrs. Rode made herself a cup of tea and sat down in the drawing-room to await his return.

Adjoining the back of the house is a conservatory, the inner door of which leads to the drawing room. It was there that Rode eventually found his wife when he returned. There were signs of a struggle, and certain inexpensive articles of jewelry were missing from the body. The confusion in the conservatory was terrible. Fortunately there had been a fresh fall of snow on Wednesday afternoon, and detectives from Dorchester were examining the footprints and other traces early on Thursday morning. Mr. Rode had been treated for shock at Dorchester Central Hospital. The police wished to interview a woman from the adjacent village of Pylle who was locally known as "Mad Janie" on account of her eccentric and solitary habits. Mrs. Rode, who was well known in Carne for her energetic work on behalf of the International Refugee Year, had apparently shown a charitable interest in her welfare, and she had vanished without trace since the night of the murder. The police were currently of the opinion that the murderer had caught sight of Mrs. Rode through the drawing-room window (she had not drawn the curtains) and that Mrs. Rode had admitted the murderer at the front door in the belief that it was her husband returning from Mr. Fielding's house. The Home Office pathologist had been asked to conduct a post-mortem examination.

The other reports were not so restrained: "Murder most foul has desecrated the hallowed playing fields of Carne" one article began, and another, "Science teacher discovers murdered wife in blood-spattered conservatory." A third screamed, "Mad woman sought in Carne murder." With an expression of distaste, Smiley screwed up all the newspapers except the *Guardian* and *The Times* and tossed them onto the luggage rack.

He changed at Yeovil for a local line to Sturminster, Okeford and Carne. It was something after eleven o'clock when he finally arrived at Carne station.

He telephoned the hotel from the station and sent his luggage ahead by taxi. The Sawley Arms was only full at Commemoration and on St. Andrew's Day. Most of the year it was empty; sitting like a prim Victorian lady, its slate roof in the mauve of half mourning, on ill tended lawns midway between the station and Carne Abbey.

Snow still lay on the ground, but the day was fine and dry, and Smiley decided to walk into the town and arrange to meet the police officer conducting the investigation of the murder. He left the station, with its foretaste of Victorian austerity, and walked along the avenue of bare trees which led towards the great Abbey tower, flat and black against the colourless winter sky. He crossed the Abbey Close, a serene and beautiful square of mediaeval houses, the roofs snow-covered, the white lawns shaded with pin strokes of grass. As he passed the west door of the Abbey, the soft snow creaking where he trod, the clock high above him struck the half-hour, and two knights on horseback rode out from their little castle over the door, and slowly raised their lances to each other in salute. Then, as if it were all part of the same clockwork mechanism, other doors all round the Close opened too, releasing swarms of black-coated boys who stampeded across the snow towards the Abbey. One boy passed so close that his gown brushed against Smiley's sleeve. Smiley called to him as he ran past:

"What's going on?"

"Sext," shouted the boy in reply, and was gone.

He passed the main entrance to the school and came at once upon the municipal part of the town, a lugubrious nineteenth-century fairyland in local stone, stitched together by a complexity of Gothic chimneys and crenel windows. Here was the town hall, and beside it, with the flag of St. George floating at its masthead, the Carne Constabulary Headquarters, built ninety years ago to withstand the onslaughts of archery and battering rams.

He gave his name to the Duty Sergeant, and asked to see the officer investigating the death of Mrs. Rode. The Sergeant, an elderly, inscrutable man, addressed himself to the telephone with a certain formality, as if he were about to perform a difficult conjuring trick. To Smiley's surprise, he was told that Inspector Rigby would be pleased to see him at once, and a police cadet was summoned to show him the way. He was led at a spanking pace up the wide staircase in the centre of the hall, and in a matter of moments found himself before the Inspector.

He was a very short man, and very broad. He could have been a Celt from the tin-mines of Cornwall or the collieries of Wales. His dark grey hair was cut very close; it came to a point in the centre of his brow like a devil's cap. His hands were large and powerful, he had the trunk and stance of a wrestler, but he spoke slowly, with a Dorset burr to his soft voice. Smiley quickly noticed that he had one quality rare among small men: the quality of openness. Though his eyes were dark and bright and the movements of his body swift, he imparted a feeling of honesty and straight dealing.

"Ben Sparrow rang me this morning, sir. I'm very pleased you've come. I believe you've got a letter for me."

Rigby looked at Smiley thoughtfully over his desk, and decided that he liked what he saw. He had got around in the war and had heard a little, just a very little, of the work of George Smiley's service. If Ben said Smiley was all right, that was good enough for him—or almost. But Ben had said more than that.

"Looks like a frog, dresses like a bookie, and has a brain I'd give my eyes for. Had a very nasty war. Very nasty indeed."

Well, he looked like a frog, right enough. Short and stubby, round spectacles with thick lenses that made his eyes big. And his clothes *were* odd. Expensive, mind, you could see that. But his jacket seemed to drape where there wasn't any room for drape. What did surprise Rigby was his shyness. Rigby had expected someone a little brash, a little too smooth for Carne, whereas Smiley had an earnest formality of manner which appealed to Rigby's conservative taste.

Smiley took the letter from his wallet and put it on the desk, while Rigby extracted an old pair of gold-rimmed spectacles from a battered metal case and adjusted the ends carefully over his ears.

"I don't know if Ben explained," said Smiley, "but this letter was sent to the correspondence section of a small Nonconformist journal to which Mrs. Rode subscribed."

"And Miss Fellowship is the lady who brought you the letter?"

"No; her name is Brimley. She is the editor of the magazine. Fellowship is just a pen-name for the correspondence column."

The brown eyes rested on him for a moment.

"When did she receive this letter?"

"Yesterday, the seventeenth. Thursday's the day they go to press, their busy day. The afternoon mail doesn't get opened till the evening, usually. This was opened about six o'clock, I suppose."

"And she brought it straight to you?"

"Yes."

"Why?"

"She worked for me during the war, in my department. She was reluctant to go straight to the police—I was the only person she could think of who wasn't a policeman," he added stupidly. "Who could help, I mean."

"May I ask what you yourself, sir, do for a living?"

"Nothing much. A little private research on seventeenth-century Germany." It seemed a very silly answer.

Rigby didn't seem bothered.

"What's this earlier letter she talks about?"

Smiley offered him the second envelope, and again the big, square hand received it.

"It appears she won this competition," Smiley explained. "That was her winning entry. I gather she comes from a family which has subscribed to the magazine since its foundation. That's why Miss Brimley was less inclined to regard the letter as nonsense. Not that it follows."

"Not that what follows?"

"I meant that the fact that her family had subscribed to a journal for fifty years does not logically affect the possibility that she was unbalanced."

Rigby nodded, as if he saw the point, but Smiley had an uncomfortable feeling that he did not.

"Ah," said Rigby, with a slow smile. "Women, eh?"

Smiley, completely bewildered, gave a little laugh. Rigby was looking at him thoughtfully.

"Know any of the staff, here, do you, sir?"

"Only Mr. Terence Fielding. We met at an Oxford dinner some time ago. I thought I'd call round and see him. I knew his brother pretty well."

Rigby appeared to stiffen slightly at the mention of Fielding, but he said nothing, and Smiley went on:

"It was Fielding I rang when Miss Brimley brought me the letter. He told me the news. That was last night."

"I see."

They looked at one another again in silence. Smiley discomfited and slightly comic, Rigby appraising him, wondering how much to say.

"How long are you staying?" he said at last.

"I don't know," Smiley replied. "Miss Brimley wanted to come herself, but she has her paper to run. She attached great importance, you see, to doing all she could for Mrs. Rode, even though she was dead. Because she was a subscriber, I mean. I promised to see that the letter arrived quickly in the right hands. I don't imagine there's much else I can do. I shall probably stay on for a day or two just to have a word with Fielding . . . go to the funeral, I suppose. I've booked in at the Sawley Arms."

"Fine hotel, that."

Rigby put his spectacles carefully back into their case and dropped the case into a drawer.

"Funny place, Carne. There's a big gap between the Town and Gown, as we say; neither side knows nor likes the other. It's fear that does it, fear and ignorance. It makes it hard in a case like this. Oh, I can call on Mr. Fielding and Mr. D'Arcy and they say, 'Good day, Sergeant,' and give me a cup of tea in the kitchen, but I can't get among them. They've got their own community, see, and no one outside it can get in. No gossip in the pubs, no contacts, nothing . . . just cups of tea and bits of seed cake, and being called Sergeant." Rigby laughed suddenly, and Smiley with him in relief. "There's a lot I'd like to ask them, a lot of things; who liked the Rodes and who didn't, whether Mr. Rode's a good teacher and whether his wife fitted with the others. I've got all the facts I want, but I've got no clothes to hang on them." He looked at Smiley expectantly. There was a very long silence.

"If you want me to help, I'd be delighted," said Smiley at last. "But give me the facts first."

"Stella Rode was murdered between about ten past eleven and quarter to twelve on the night of Wednesday the sixteenth. She must have been struck fifteen to twenty times with a cosh or bit of piping or something. It was a terrible murder . . . terrible. There are marks all over her body. At a guess I would say she came from the drawing room to the front door to answer the bell or something, when she opened the door she was struck down and dragged to the conservatory. The conservatory door was unlocked, see?"

"I see. . . . It's odd that he should have known that, isn't it?"

"The murderer may have been hiding there already: we can't tell from the prints just there. He was wearing boots—wellington boots, size 10½. We would guess from the spacing of the footprints in the garden that he was about six foot tall. When he had got her to the conservatory he must have hit her again and again—mainly on the head. There's a lot of what we call travelled blood in the conservatory, that's to say, blood spurted from an open artery. There's no sign of that anywhere else."

"And no sign of it on her husband?"

"I'll come to that later, but the short answer is, no." He paused a moment and continued:

"Now, I said there were footprints, and so there were. The murderer came through the back garden. Where he came from and went to, Heaven alone knows. You see, there are no tracks leading away—not wellingtons. None at all. Of course, it's possible the outgoing tracks followed the path to the front gate and got lost in all the to-ing and fro-ing later that night. But I don't think we'd have lost them even then." He glanced at Smiley, then went on:

"He left one thing behind him in the conservatory—an old cloth belt, navy blue, from a cheap overcoat by the look of it. We're working on that now."

"Was she . . . robbed or anything?"

"No sign of interference. She was wearing a string of green beads round her neck, and they've gone, and it looks as though he tried to get the rings off her finger, but they were too tight." He paused.

"I need hardly tell you that we've had reports from every corner of the country about tall men in blue overcoats and gumboots. But none of them had wings as far as I know. Or seven-league boots for jumping from the conservatory to the road."

They paused, while a police cadet brought in tea on a tray. He put it on the desk, looked at Smiley out of the corner of his eye and decided to let the Inspector pour out. He guided the teapot round so that the handle was towards Rigby and withdrew. Smiley was amused by the immaculate condition of the tray cloth, by the matching china and the tea-strainer, laid before them by the enormous hands of the cadet. Rigby poured out the tea and they drank for a moment in silence. There was, Smiley reflected, something devastatingly competent about Rigby. The very ordinariness of the man and his room identified him with the society he protected. The nondescript furniture, the wooden filing cupboards, the bare walls, the archaic telephone with its separate ear-piece, the brown frieze round the wall and the brown paint on the door, the glistening linoleum and the faint smell of carbolic, the burbling gas-fire and the calendar from the Prudential—these were the evidence of rectitude and moderation; their austerity gave comfort and reassurance. Rigby continued:

"Rode went back to Fielding's house for the examination papers. Fielding confirms that, of course. He arrived at Fielding's house at about 11.35, near as Fielding can say. He hardly spent any time there at all—just collected his papers at the door—they were in a small writing-case he uses for carrying exercise books. He doesn't remember whether he saw anyone on the road. He thinks a bicycle overtook him, but he can't be sure. If we take Rode's word for it, he walked straight home. When he got there he rang the bell. He was wearing a dinner jacket and so he hadn't got his key with him. His wife was expecting him to ring the bell, you see. That's the devil of it. It was a moonlit night, mind, and snow on the ground, so you could see a mighty long way. He called her, but she didn't answer. Then he saw the footprints going round to the side of the house. Not just footprints, but blood marks and the snow all churned up where the body had been dragged to the conservatory. But he didn't know it was blood in the moonlight, it just showed up dark, and Rode said afterwards he thought it was the dirty water from the gutters running over on to the path.

"He followed the prints round until he came to the conservatory. It was darker in there and he fumbled for the light switch, but it didn't work."

"Did he light a match?"

"No, he didn't have any. He's a non-smoker. His wife didn't approve of smoking. He moved forward from the door. The conservatory walls are mainly glass except for the bottom three feet, but the roof is tiled. The moon was high that night, and not much light got in at all, except through the partition window between the drawing room and the conservatory—but she'd only had the little table light on in the drawing-room. So he groped his way forward, talking all the time, calling Stella, his wife. As he went, he tripped over something and nearly fell. He knelt down and felt with his hands, up and down her body. He realised that his hands were covered in blood. He doesn't remember much after that, but there's a senior master living a hundred yards up the road—Mr. D'Arcy his name is, lives with his sister, and he heard him screaming on the road. D'Arcy went out to him. Rode had blood all over his hands and face and seemed to be out of his mind. D'Arcy rang the police and I got there at about one o'clock that morning. I've seen some nasty things in my time, but this is the worst. Blood everywhere. Whoever killed her must have been covered in it. There's an outside tap against the conservatory wall. The tap had been turned on, probably by the murderer to rinse his hands. The boffins have found traces of blood in the snow underneath it. The tap was lagged recently by Rode I gather. . . ."

"And fingerprints?" Smiley asked. "What about them?"

"Mr. Rode's were everywhere. On the floor, the walls and windows, on the body itself. But there were other prints; smudges of blood, little more, made with a gloved hand probably."

"And they were the murderer's?"

"They had been made *before* Rode made his. In some cases Rode's prints were partly superimposed on the glove prints."

Smiley was silent for a moment.

"These examination papers he went back for. Were they as important as all that?"

"Yes. I gather they were. Up to a point anyway. The marks had to be handed in to Mr. D'Arcy by midday on Friday."

"But why did he take them to Fielding's in the first place?"

"He didn't. He'd been invigilating exams all afternoon and the papers were handed in to him at six o'clock. He put them in his little case and had them taken to Fielding's by a boy—head boy in Mr. Fielding's house, name of Perkins. Rode was on Chapel duty last week, so he didn't have time to return home before dinner."

"Where did he change then?"

"In the Tutors' Robing Room, next to the Common Room. There are facilities there, mainly for games tutors who live some distance from Carne."

"The boy who brought this case to Fielding's house—who was he?"

"I can't tell you much more than I've said. His name is Perkins; he's head of Mr. Fielding's house. Fielding has spoken to him and confirmed Rode's statement. . . . House tutors are very possessive about their boys, you know . . . don't like them to be spoken to by rough policemen." Rigby seemed to be slightly upset.

"I see," Smiley said at last, helplessly, and then: "But how do you explain the letter?"

"It isn't only the letter we've got to explain."

Smiley looked at him sharply.

"What do you mean?"

"I mean," said Rigby slowly, "that Mrs. Rode did several pretty queer things in the last few weeks."

IV

Town And Gown

"Mrs. Rode was Chapel, of course," Rigby continued, "and we've quite a community in Carne. Truth to tell," he added with a slow smile, "my wife belongs to it.

"A couple of weeks ago our Minister called round to see me. It was in the evening, about half past six, I suppose. I was just thinking of going home, see. He walked in here and sat himself down where you're sitting now. He's a big fellow, the Minister, a fine man; comes from up North, where Mrs. Rode came from. Cardew, his name is."

"The Mr. Cardew in the letter?"

"That's him. He knew all about Mrs. Rode's family before the Rodes ever came here. Glaston's quite a name up North, and Mr. Cardew was very pleased when he heard that Stella Rode was Mr. Glaston's daughter; very pleased indeed. Mrs. Rode came to the Tabernacle regular as clockwork, you can imagine, and they like to see that round here. My wife was pleased as Punch, I can tell you. It was the first time, I suppose, that anyone from the School had done that. Most of the Chapel people here are tradespeople—what we call the locals." Rigby smiled again. "It isn't often that town and gown come together, so to speak. Not here."

"How about her husband? Was he Chapel too?"

"Well, he had been, so she told Mr. Cardew. Mr.

33

Rode was born and bred in Branxome, and all his family were Chapel people. That's how Mr. and Mrs. Rode first met, I gather—at Branxome Tabernacle. Ever been there, have you? A fine church Branxome, right up on the hill there, overlooking the sea."

Smiley shook his head and Rigby's wide brown eyes rested on him thoughtfully for a moment.

"You should," he said, "you should go and see that. It seems," he continued, "that Mr. Rode turned Church of England when he came to Carne. Even tried to persuade his wife to do the same. They're very strong at the School. I heard that from my wife, as a matter of fact. I never let her gossip as a rule, being a policeman's wife and that, but Mr. Cardew told her that himself."

"I see," said Smiley.

"Well now, Cardew came and saw me. He was all worried and bothered with himself. He didn't know what he should make of it, but he wanted to talk to me as a friend and not as a policeman." Rigby looked sour, "When people say that to me, I always know that they want to talk to me as a policeman. Then he told me his story. Mrs. Rode had called to see him that afternoon. He'd been out visiting a farmer's wife over in Okeford and didn't come home until half past five or thereabouts, so Mrs. Cardew had had to talk to her and hold the fort until the Minister came home. Mrs. Rode was white as a sheet, sitting very still by the fire. As soon as the Minister arrived, Mrs. Cardew left them alone and Stella Rode started talking about her husband."

He paused. "She said Mr. Rode was going to kill her. In the long nights. She seemed to have a kind of fixation about being murdered in the long nights. Cardew didn't take it too seriously at first, but thinking about it afterwards, he decided to let me know."

Smiley looked at him sharply.

"He couldn't make out what she meant. He thought she was out of her mind. He's a down-to-earth man, see, although he's a Minister. I think he was probably a bit too firm with her. He asked her what put this dreadful thought into her head, and she began to weep. Not hysterical, apparently, but just crying quietly to herself. He tried to calm her down, promised to help her any way he could, and asked her again what had given her this idea. She just shook her head, then got up, walked over to the door, still shaking her head in despair. She turned to him, and he thought she was going to say something, but she didn't. She just left."

"How very curious," said Smiley, "that she lied about that in her letter. She went out of her way to say she *hadn't* told Cardew."

Rigby shrugged his great shoulders.

"If you'll pardon me," he said, "I'm in a darned awkward position. The Chief Constable would sooner cut his throat than call in Scotland Yard. He wants an arrest and he wants one quick. We've got enough clues to cover a Christmas tree; footprints, time of the murder, indication of murderer's clothing and even the weapon itself."

Smiley looked at him in surprise.

"You've *found* the weapon, then?"

Rigby hesitated. "Yes, we've found it. There's hardly a soul knows this, sir, and I'll trouble you to remember that. We found it the morning after the murder, four miles north of Carne on the Okeford road, tossed into a ditch. Eighteen inches of what they call coaxial cable. Know what that is, do you? It comes in all sizes, but this piece is about two inches in diameter. It has a copper rod running down the middle and the plastic insulation between the rod and the outer cover. There was blood on it: Stella Rode's blood group, and hairs from her head, stuck to the blood. We're keeping that very dark indeed. By the Grace of God, it was found by one of our own men. It pinpoints the line of the murderer's departure."

"There's no doubt, I suppose, that it *is* the weapon?" Smiley asked lamely.

"We found particles of copper in the wounds on the body."

"It's odd, isn't it," Smiley suggested reflectively, "that the murderer should have carried the weapon so far before getting rid of it? Specially if he was walking.

You'd think he'd want to get rid of it as soon as he could."

"It is odd. Very odd. The Okeford road runs beside the canal for half of those four miles; he could have pitched the cable into the canal anywhere along there. We'd never have been the wiser."

"Was the cable old?"

"Not particularly. Just standard type. It could have come from almost anywhere." Rigby hesitated a minute, then burst out:

"Look, sir, this is what I am trying to say. The circumstances of this case demand a certain type of investigation: wide-scale search, detailed laboratory work, mass enquiry. That's what the Chief wants, and he's right. We've no case against the husband at all, and to be frank he's precious little use to us. He seems a bit lost, a bit vague, contradicting himself on little things that don't matter, like the date of his marriage or the name of his doctor. It's shock, of course, I've seen it before. I know all about your letter, sir, and it's damned odd, but if you can tell me how he could have produced wellington boots out of a hat and got rid of them afterwards, battered his wife to death without leaving more than a few smudges of blood on himself, and got the weapon four miles from the scene of the crime, all within ten minutes of being at Fielding's house, I'll be grateful to you. We're looking for a stranger, six foot tall, wearing newish Dunlop Wellington boots size 10½, leather gloves and an old blue overcoat stained with blood. A man who travels on foot, who was in the area of North Fields between 11.10 and 11.45 on the night of the murder, who left in the direction of Okeford, taking with him one and a half feet of coaxial cable, a string of green beads and an imitation diamond clip, valued at twenty-three and six. We're looking for a maniac, a man who kills for pleasure or the price of a meal." Rigby paused, smiled wistfully and added, "Who can fly fifty feet through the air. But with information like this how else should we spend our time? What else can we look for? I can't put men on to chasing shadows when there's work like that to be done."

"I understand that."

"But I'm an old policeman, Mr. Smiley, and I like to know what I'm about. I don't like looking for people I can't believe in, and I don't like being cut off from witnesses. I like to meet people and talk to them, nose about here and there, get to know the country. But I can't do that, not at the school. Do you follow me? So we've got to rely on laboratories, tracker dogs and nationwide searches, but somehow in my bones I don't think it's altogether one of those cases."

"I read in the paper about a woman, a Mad Janie . . ."

"I'm coming to that. Mrs. Rode was a kindly woman, easy to talk to. I always found her so, anyway. Some of the women at Chapel took against her, but you know what women are. It seems she got friendly with this Janie creature. Janie came begging, selling herbs and charms at the back door; you know the kind of thing. She's queer, talks to birds and all that. She lives in a disused Norman chapel over to Pylle. Stella Rode used to give her food and clothes—the poor soul was often as not half-starved. Now Janie's disappeared. She was seen early Wednesday night on the lane towards North Fields and hasn't been seen since. That don't mean a thing. These people come and go in their own way. They'll be all over the neighbourhood for years, then one day they're gone like snow in the fire. They've died in a ditch, maybe, or they've took ill and crept away like a cat. Janie's not the only queer one round here. There's a lot of excitement because we found a spare set of footprints running along the fringe of trees at the far end of the garden. They were a woman's prints by the look of them, and at one point they come quite close to the conservatory. Could be a gypsy or a beggar woman. Could be anything, but I expect it's Janie right enough. I hope to Heaven it was, sir; we could do with an eyewitness, even a mad one."

Smiley stood up. As they shook hands, Rigby said, "Goodbye, sir. Ring me any time, any time at all." He scribbled a telephone number on the pad in front of him, tore off the sheet and gave it to Smiley. "That's my

home number." He showed Smiley to the door, seemed
to hesitate, then he said, "You're not a Carnian yourself
by any chance, are you, sir?"

"Good heavens, no."

Again Rigby hesitated. "Our Chief's a Carnian.
Ex-Indian Army. Brigadier Havelock. This is his last
year. He's very interested in this case. Doesn't like me
messing around the school. Won't have it."

"I see."

"He wants an arrest quickly."

"And outside Carne, I suppose?"

"Goodbye, Mr. Smiley. Don't forget to ring me.
Oh, another thing I should have mentioned. That bit of
cable . . ."

"Yes?"

"Mr. Rode used a length of the same stuff in a
demonstration lecture on elementary electronics. Mis-
laid it about three weeks ago."

Smiley walked slowly back to his hotel.

My dear Brim,

*As soon as I arrived I handed your letter
over to the C.I.D. man in charge of the case—it
was Rigby, as Ben had supposed; he looks like a
mixture of Humpty-Dumpty and a Cornish elf—
very short and broad—and I don't think he's anyone's fool.*

*To begin at the middle—our letter didn't
have quite the effect we expected; Stella Rode evidently told Cardew, the local Baptist Minister,
two weeks ago, that her husband was trying to
kill her in the long nights, whatever they are. As
for the circumstances of the murder—the account
in the* Guardian *is substantially correct.*

*In fact, the more Rigby told me, the less likely
it became that she was killed by her husband. Almost everything pointed away from him. Quite
apart from motive, there is the location of the
weapon, the footprints in the snow (which indicate a tall man in wellingtons), the presence of
unidentified glove-prints in the conservatory. Add
to that the strongest argument of all: whoever
killed her must have been covered in blood—the*

conservatory was a dreadful sight, Rigby tells me. Of course, there was blood on Rode when he was picked up by his colleague in the lane, but only smears which could have resulted from stumbling over the body in the dark. Incidentally, the foot-prints only go into the garden and not out.

As things stand at the moment, there is, as Rigby points out, only one interpretation—the murderer was a stranger, a tramp, a madman per-haps, who killed her for pleasure or for her jewel-ery (which was worthless) and made off along the Okeford road, throwing the weapon into a ditch. (But why carry it four miles—and why not throw it into the canal the other side of the ditch? The Okeford road crosses Okemoor, which is all cross-dyked to prevent flooding.) If this interpretation is correct, then I suppose we attribute Stella's let-ter and her interview with Cardew to a persecuted mind, or the premonition of death, depending on whether we're superstitious. If that is so, it is the most monstrous coincidence I have ever heard of. Which brings me to my final point.

I rather gathered from what Rigby didn't say that his Chief Constable was treading on his tail, urging him to scour the country for tramps in bloodstained blue overcoats (you remember the belt). Rigby, of course, has no alternative but to follow the signs and do as his Chief expects—but he is clearly uneasy about something—either something he hasn't told me, or something he just feels in his bones. I think he was sincere when he asked me to tell him anything I found out about the School end—the Rodes themselves, the way they fitted in, and so on. Carne's monastery walls are still pretty high, he feels. . . .

So I'll just sniff around a bit, I think, and see what goes on. I rang Fielding when I got back from the police station and he's asked me to sup-per tonight. I'll write again as soon as I have any-thing to tell you.

George.

Having carefully sealed the envelope, pressing down the corners with his thumbs, Smiley locked his

door and made his way down the wide marble staircase,
treading carefully on the meagre coconut matting that
ran down the centre. There was a red wooden letter box
in the hall for the use of residents, but Smiley, being a
cautious man, avoided it. He walked to the pillar box at
the corner of the road, posted his letter and wondered
what to do about lunch. There were, of course, the
sandwiches and coffee provided by Miss Brimley. Reluctantly he returned to the hotel. It was full of journalists, and Smiley hated journalists. It was also cold, and
he hated the cold. And there was something very familiar about sandwiches in a hotel bedroom.

V

Cat And Dog

It was just after seven o'clock that evening when George
Smiley climbed the steps which led up to the front door
of Mr. Terence Fielding's house. He rang, and was admitted to the hall by a little plump woman in her middle
fifties. To his right a log fire burned warmly on a pile of
wood ash and above him he was vaguely aware of a
minstrel gallery and a mahogany staircase, which rose
in a spiral to the top of the house. Most of the light
seemed to come from the fire, and Smiley could see that
the walls around him were hung with a great number
of paintings of various styles and periods, and the
chimney-piece was laden with all manner of *objets
d'art*. With an involuntary shudder, he noticed that neither the fire nor the pictures quite succeeded in banish-
ing the faint smell of school—of polish bought whole-
sale, of cocoa and community cooking. Corridors led
from the hall, and Smiley observed that the lower part
of each wall was painted a dark brown or green according to the inflexible rule of school decorators. From one
of these corridors the enormous figure of Mr. Terence
Fielding emerged.

He advanced on Smiley, massive and genial, with
his splendid mane of grey hair falling anyhow across his
forehead, and his gown billowing behind him.

"Smiley? Ah! You've met True, have you—Miss

Truebody, my housekeeper? Marvellous this snow, isn't it? Pure Breughel! Seen the boys skating by the Eyot? Marvellous sight! Black suits, coloured scarves, pale sun; all there, isn't it, all there! Breughel to the life. Marvellous!" He took Smiley's coat and flung it on to a decrepit deal chair with a rush seat which stood in the corner of the hall.

"You like that chair—you recognise it?"

"I don't think I do," Smiley replied in some confusion.

"Ah, you should, you know, you should! Had it made in Provence before the war. Little carpenter I knew. Place it now? Facsimile of Van Gogh's yellow chair; some people recognise it." He led the way down a corridor and into a large comfortable study adorned with Dutch tiles, small pieces of Renaissance sculpture, mysterious bronzes, china dogs and unglazed vases; and Fielding himself towering magnificent among them.

As senior housemaster of Carne, Fielding wore, in place of the customary academic dress, a wonderful confection of heavy black skirts and legal bib, like a monk in evening dress. All this imparted a suggestion of clerical austerity in noted contrast to the studied flamboyance of his personality. Evidently conscious of this, he sought to punctuate the solemnity of his uniform and give to it a little of his own temperament, by adorning it with flowers carefully chosen from his garden. He had scandalised the tailors of Carne, whose frosted windows carried the insignia of royal households, by having buttonholes let into his gown. These he would fill according to his mood with anything from hibernia to bluebells. This evening he wore a rose, and from its freshness Smiley deduced that he had this minute put it into place, having ordered it specially.

"Sherry wine or Madeira?"

"Thank you; a glass of sherry."

"Tart's drink, Madeira," Fielding called, as he poured from a decanter, "but boys like it. Perhaps that's why. They're frightful flirts." He handed Smiley a glass and added, with a dramatic modification of his voice: "We're all rather subdued at the moment by this dreadful business. We've never had anything quite like it, you know. Have you seen the evening papers?"

"No, I'm afraid I haven't. But the Sawley Arms is packed with journalists of course."

"They've really gone to town. They've got the Army out in Hampshire, playing about with mine-detectors. God knows what they expect to find."

"How have the boys taken it?"

"They adore it! My own house has been particularly fortunate, of course, because the Rodes were dining here that night. Some oaf from the police even wanted to question one of my boys."

"Indeed," said Smiley innocently. "What on earth about?"

"Oh, God knows," Fielding replied abruptly, and then, changing the subject, he asked, "You knew my brother well, didn't you? He talked about you, you know."

"Yes, I knew Adrian very well. We were close friends."

"In the war, too?"

"Yes."

"Were you in his crowd, then?"

"What crowd?"

"Steed, Asprey, Jebedee. All those people."

"Yes."

"I never really heard how he died. Did you?"

"No."

"We didn't see much of one another in later years, Adrian and I. Being a fraud, I can't afford to be seen beside the genuine article," Fielding declared, with something of his earlier panache. Smiley was spared the embarrassment of a reply by a quiet knock at the door, and a tall red-haired boy came timidly into the room.

"I've called the Adsum, sir, if you're ready, sir."

"Damn," said Fielding, emptying his glass. "Prayers." He turned to Smiley.

"Meet Perkins, my head prefect. Musical genius, but a problem in the schoolroom. That right, Tim? Stay here or come as you like. It only lasts ten minutes."

"Rather less tonight, sir," said Perkins. "It's the Nunc Dimittis."

"Thank God for small mercies," Fielding declared, tugging briefly at his bib, as he led Smiley at a spanking pace out into the corridor and across the hall, with Perkins stalking along behind them. Fielding was speaking all the time without bothering to turn his head:

"I'm glad you've chosen this evening to come. I never entertain on Saturdays as a rule because everyone else does, though none of us quite knows what to do about entertaining at the moment. Felix D'Arcy will be coming tonight, but that's hardly entertaining. D'Arcy's a professional. Incidentally, we normally dress in the evening, but it doesn't matter."

Smiley's heart sank. They turned a corner and entered another corridor.

"We have prayers at all hours here. The Master's revived the seven Day Hours for the Offices: Prime, Terce, Sext and so on. A surfeit during the Half, abstinence during the holidays, that's the system, like games. Useful in the house for roll-calls, too." He led the way down yet another corridor, flung open a double door at the end of it and marched straight into the dining-room, his gown filling gracefully behind him. The boys were waiting for him.

"More sherry? What did you think of prayers? They sing quite nicely, don't they? One or two good tenors. We tried some plainsong last Half; quite good, really quite good. D'Arcy will be here soon. He's a frightful toad. Looks like a Sickert model fifty years after—all trousers and collar. However, you're lucky his sister isn't accompanying him. She's worse!"

"What's his subject?" They were back in Fielding's study.

"Subject! I'm afraid we don't have subjects here. None of us has read a word on any subject since we left University." He lowered his voice and added darkly, "That's if we *went* to University. D'Arcy teaches French. D'Arcy is senior tutor by election, bachelor by profession, sublimated pansy by inclination . . ." he was standing quite still now, his head thrown back and his right hand stretched out towards Smiley, ". . . and his subject is other people's shortcomings. He is principally, however, self-appointed majordomo of Carne protocol. If you wear a gown on a bicycle, reply incorrectly to an invitation, make a fault in the *placement* of your dinner guests or speak of a colleague as 'Mister,' D'Arcy will find you out and admonish you."

"What are the duties of Senior Tutor, then?" Smiley asked, just for something to say.

"He's the referee between the classics and the scientists; arranges the timetable and vets the exam. results. But principally, poor man, he must reconcile the Arts with the Sciences." He shook his head sagely. "And it takes a better man than D'Arcy to do that. Not, mind you," he added wearily, "that it makes the least difference who wins the extra hour on Friday evenings. Who cares? Not the boys, poor dears, that's certain."

Fielding talked on, at random and always in superlatives, sometimes groping in the air with his hand as if to catch the more elusive metaphors; now of his colleagues with caustic derision, now of boys with compassion if not with understanding; now of the Arts with fervour—and the studied bewilderment of a lonely disciple.

"Carne isn't a school. It's a sanatorium for intellectual lepers. The symptoms began when we came down from University; a gradual putrefication of our intellectual extremities. From day to day our minds die, our spirits atrophy and rot. We watch the process in one another, hoping to forget it in ourselves." He paused, and looked reflectively at his hands.

"In me the process is complete. You see before you a dead soul, and Carne is the body I live in." Much pleased by this confession, Fielding held out his great arms so that the sleeves of his gown resembled the wings of a giant bat, "the Vampire of Carne," he declared, bowing deeply. "Alcoholique et poete!" A bellow of laughter followed this display.

Smiley was fascinated by Fielding, by his size, his voice, the wanton inconstancy of his temperament, by his whole big-screen style; he found himself attracted and repelled by this succession of contradictory poses; he wondered whether he was supposed to take part in the performance, but Fielding seemed so dazzled by the footlights that he was indifferent to the audience behind them. The more Smiley watched, the more elusive seemed the character he was trying to comprehend: changeful but sterile, daring but fugitive; colourful, unbounded, ingenuous, yet deceitful and perverse. Smiley began to wish he could acquire the material facts of Fielding—his means, his ambitions and disappointments.

His reverie was interrupted by Miss Truebody. Felix D'Arcy had arrived.

No candles, and a cold supper admirably done by Miss Truebody. Not claret, but hock, passed round like port. And at last, at long last, Fielding mentioned Stella Rode.

They had been talking rather dutifully of the Arts and the Sciences. This would have been dull (for it was uninformed) had not D'Arcy constantly been goaded by Fielding, who seemed anxious to exhibit D'Arcy in his worst light. D'Arcy's judgements of people and problems were largely coloured by what he considered "seemly" (a favourite word) and by an effeminate malice towards his colleagues. After a while Fielding asked who was replacing Rode during his absence, to which D'Arcy said, "No one," and added unctuously:

"It was a terrible shock to the community, this affair."

"Nonsense," Fielding retorted. "Boys love disaster. The further we are from death the more attractive it seems. They find the whole affair most exhilarating."

"The publicity has been most unseemly," said D'Arcy, "most. I think that has been prominent in the minds of many of us in the Common Room." He turned to Smiley:

"The press, you know, is a constant worry here. In the past it could never have happened. Formerly our great families and institutions were not subjected to this intrusion. No, indeed not. But today all that is changed. Many of us are compelled to subscribe to the cheaper newspapers for this very reason. One Sunday newspaper mentioned no fewer than four of Hecht's old boys in one edition. All of them in an unseemly context, I may say. And of course such papers never fail to mention that the boy is a Carnian. You know, I suppose, that we have the young prince here. (I myself have the honour to supervise his French studies.) The young Sawley is also at Carne. The activity of the press during his parents' divorce suit was deplorable. Quite deplorable. The Master wrote to the Press Council, you know. I drafted the letter myself. But on this tragic occasion they have excelled themselves. We even had the press at Compline last night, you know, waiting for the Special Prayer. They occupied the whole of the two rear pews on the west side. Hecht was doing Chapel Duty and tried to have them removed." He paused, raised his eyebrows in gentle reproach and smiled. "He had no business to, of course, but that never stopped the good Hecht." He turned to Smiley. "One of our *athletic* brethren," he explained.

"Stella was too common for you, Felix, wasn't she?"

"Not at all," said D'Arcy quickly. "I would not have you say that of me, Terence. I am by no means discriminatory in the matter of class; merely of manners. I grant you, in that particular field, I found her wanting."

.. "In many ways she was just what we needed," Fielding continued, addressing Smiley and ignoring D'Arcy. "She was everything we're forced to ignore— she was red-brick, council estates, new towns, the very antithesis of Carne! He turned suddenly to D'Arcy and said, "But to you, Felix, she was just bad form."

"Not at all; merely unsuitable."

Fielding turned to Smiley in despair.

"Look," he said. "We talk academic here, you know, wear academic dress and hold high table dinners in the Common Room; we have long graces in Latin that none of us can translate. We go to the Abbey and the wives sit in the hencoop in their awful hats. But it's a charade. It means nothing."

D'Arcy smiled wanly.

"I cannot believe, my dear Terence, that anyone who keeps such an excellent table as yourself can have so low an opinion of the refinements of social conduct." He looked to Smiley for support and Smiley dutifully echoed the compliment. "Besides, we know Terence of old at Carne. I am afraid we are accustomed to his roar."

"I know why you disliked that woman, Felix. She was honest, and Carne has no defence against that kind of honesty."

D'Arcy suddenly became very angry indeed.

"Terence, I will not have you say this. I simply will not have it. I feel I have a certain duty at Carne, as indeed we all have, to restore and maintain those standards of behaviour which suffered so sadly in the war. I am sensible that this determination has made me on more than one occasion unpopular. But such comment or advice as I offer is never—I beg you to notice this—is *never* directed against personalities, only against behaviour, against unseemly lapses in conduct. I will acknowledge that more than once I was compelled to address Rode on the subject of his wife's conduct. That is a matter quite divorced from personalities, Terence. I will not have it said that I disliked Mrs. Rode. Such a suggestion would be disagreeable at all times, but under the present tragic circumstances it is deplorable. Mrs. Rode's own . . . background and education did not naturally prepare her for our ways; that is quite a different matter. It does, however, illustrate the point that I wish to emphasise, Terence: it was a question of enlightenment, not of criticism. Do I make myself clear?"

"Abundantly," Fielding answered drily.

"Did the other wives like her?" Smiley ventured.

"Not entirely," D'Arcy replied crisply.

"The wives! My God!" Fielding groaned, putting his hand to his brow. There was a pause.

"Her clothes, I believe, were a source of distress to some of them. She also frequented the public laundry.

This, too, would not make a favourable impression. I should add that she did not attend our church. . . ."

"Did she have any close friends among the wives?" Smiley persisted.

"I believe young Mrs. Snow took to her."

"And you say she was dining here the night she was murdered?"

"Yes," said Fielding quietly, "Wednesday. And it was Felix and his sister who took in poor Rode afterwards. . . ." He glanced at D'Arcy.

"Yes, indeed," said D'Arcy abruptly. His eyes were on Fielding, and it seemed to Smiley that something had passed between them. "We shall never forget, never. . . . Terence, if I may talk shop for just one moment, Perkins' construe is abysmal; I declare I have never seen work like it. Is he unwell? His mother is a most cultured woman, a cousin of the Samfords, I am told."

Smiley looked at him and wondered. His dinner jacket was faded, green with age. Smiley could almost hear him saying it had belonged to his grandfather. The skin of his face was so unlined that he somehow suggested fatness without being fat. His voice was pitched on one insinuating note, and he smiled all the time, whether he was speaking or not. The smile never left his smooth face, it was worked into the malleable fabric of his flesh, stretching his lips across his perfect teeth and opening the corners of his red mouth, so that it seemed to be held in place by the invisible fingers of his dentist. Yet D'Arcy's face was far from unexpressive; every mark showed. The smallest movement of his mouth or nose, the quickest glance or frown, were there to read and interpret. And he wanted to change the subject. Not away from Stella Rode (for he returned to discussing her himself a moment later), but away from the particular evening on which she died, away from the precise narration of events. And what was more, there was not a doubt in Smiley's mind that Fielding had seen it too, that in that look which passed between them was a pact of fear, a warning perhaps, so that from that moment

Fielding's manner changed, he grew sullen and preoccu-
pied, in a way that puzzled Smiley long afterwards.

D'Arcy turned to Smiley and addressed him with
cloying intimacy.

"*Do* forgive my deplorable descent into Carne gossip. You find us a little cut off, here, do you not? We
are often held to be cut off, I know. Carne is a 'Snob
School,' that is the cry. You may read it every day in
the gutter press. And yet, despite the claims of the
avant-garde," he said, glancing slyly at Fielding, "I may
say that *no one* could be less of a snob than Felix
D'Arcy." Smiley noticed his hair. It was very fine and
ginger, growing from the top and leaving his pink neck
bare.

"Take poor Rode, for instance. I certainly don't
hold Rode's background against him in any way, poor
fellow. The grammar schools do a splendid job, I am
sure. Besides, he settled down here very well. I told the
Master so. I said to him that Rode had settled down
well; he does Chapel duty quite admirably—that was
the very point I made. I hope I have played my part,
what is more, in helping him to fit in. With careful in-
struction, such people can, as I said to the Master, learn
our customs and even our manners; and the Master
agreed."

Smiley's glass was empty and D'Arcy, without con-
sulting Fielding, filled it for him from the decanter. His
hands were polished and hairless, like the hands of a
girl.

"But," he continued, "I must be honest. Mrs.
Rode did not adapt herself so willingly to our ways."
Still smiling, he sipped delicately from his glass. He
wants to put the record straight, thought Smiley.

"She would never really have fitted in at Carne;
that is my opinion—though I am sure I never voiced it
while she was alive. Her background was against her.
The fault was not hers—it was her background which,
as I say, was unfortunate. Indeed, if we may speak
frankly and in confidence, I have reason to believe it
was her past that brought about her death."

"Why do you say that?" asked Smiley quickly, and D'Arcy replied with a glance at Fielding, "It appears she was expecting to be attacked."

"My sister is devoted to dogs," D'Arcy continued. "You may know that already perhaps. King Charles spaniels are her *forte*. She took a first at the North Dorset last year and was commended at Cruft's shortly afterwards for her 'Queen of Carne.' She sells to America, you know. I dare say there are few people in the country with Dorothy's knowledge of the breed. The Master's wife found occasion to say the very same thing a week ago. Well, the Rodes were our neighbours, as you know, and Dorothy is not a person to neglect her neighbourly duties. Where duty is concerned, you will not find her discriminatory, I assure you. The Rodes also had a dog, a large mongrel, quite an intelligent animal, which they brought with them. (I have little idea where they came from, but that is another matter.) They appeared quite devoted to the dog, and I have no doubt they were. Rode took it with him to watch the football until I had occasion to advise him against it. The practice was giving rise to unseemly humour among the boys. I have found the same thing myself when exercising Dorothy's spaniels.

"I shall come to the point presently. Dorothy uses a vet called Harriman, a superior type of person who lives over toward Sturminster. A fortnight ago she sent for him. 'Queen of Carne' was coughing badly and Dorothy asked Harriman to come over. A bitch of her quality is not to be taken lightly, I assure you."

Fielding groaned, and D'Arcy continued, oblivious:

"I happened to be at home, and Harriman stayed for a cup of coffee. He is, as I say, a superior type of person. Harriman made some reference to the Rodes' dog and then the truth came out; Mrs. Rode had had the dog destroyed the previous day. She said it had bitten the postman. Some long and confused story; the Post Office would sue, the police had been round and I don't know what else. And, anyway, she said, the dog couldn't really protect, it could only warn. She had said so to Harriman, 'It wouldn't do any good.' "

"Wasn't she upset about losing the dog?" asked Smiley.

"Oh, indeed, yes. Harriman said she was in tears when she arrived. Mrs. Harriman had to give her a cup of tea. They suggested she should give the dog another chance, put it in kennels for a while, but she was adamant, quite adamant. Harriman was most perplexed. So was his wife. When they discussed it afterwards they agreed that Mrs. Rode's behaviour had not been quite normal. Not normal at all, in fact. Another curious fact was the condition of the dog: it had been maltreated, seriously so. Its back was marked as if from beatings."

"Did Harriman follow up this remark she made? About not doing any good? What did Harriman make of it?" Smiley was watching D'Arcy intently.

"She repeated it to Mrs. Harriman, but she wouldn't explain it. However, I think the explanation is obvious enough."

"Oh?" said Fielding.

D'Arcy put his head on one side and plucked coyly at the lobe of his ear.

"We all have a little of the detective in us," he said. "Dorothy and I talked it over after the—death. We decided that Stella Rode had formed some unsavoury association before coming to Carne, which had recently been revived . . . possibly against her will. Some violent ruffian—an old admirer—who would resent the improvement in her station."

"How badly was the postman bitten by the dog?" Smiley asked.

D'Arcy turned to him again.

"That is the extraordinary thing. That is the very crux of the story, my dear fellow: the postman hadn't been bitten at all. Dorothy enquired. Her whole story was an absolute string of lies from beginning to end."

They rose from the table and made their way to Fielding's study, where Miss Truebody had put the coffee. The conversation continued to wander back and

forth over Wednesday's tragedy. D'Arcy was obsessed
with the indelicacy of it all—the persistence of journalists, the insensitivity of the police, the uncertainty of
Mrs. Rode's origin, the misfortune of her husband.
Fielding was still oddly silent, sunk in his own thoughts,
from which he occasionally emerged to glance at
D'Arcy with a look of hostility. At exactly a quarter to
eleven D'Arcy pronounced himself tired, and the three
of them went into the great hall, where Miss Truebody
produced a coat for Smiley and a coat and muffler and
cap for D'Arcy. Fielding accepted D'Arcy's thanks with
a sullen nod. He turned to Smiley:

"That business you rang me about. What was it
exactly?"

"Oh—a letter from Mrs. Rode just before she was
murdered," said Smiley vaguely, "the police are handling it now, but they do not regard it as . . .
significant. Not significant at all. She seems to have had
a sort of"—he gave an embarrassed grin—"persecution
complex. Is that the expression? However, we might
discuss it some time. You must dine with me at the
Sawley before I go back. Do you come to London at
all? We might meet in London perhaps, at the end of
the Half."

D'Arcy was standing in the doorway, looking at
the new fall of snow which lay white and perfect on the
pavement before him.

"Ah," he said, with a little knowing laugh, "the
long nights, eh, Terence, the long nights."

VI

Holly For The Devil

"What are the long nights?" Smiley asked, as he and D'Arcy walked briskly away from Fielding's house through the new snow towards the Abbey Close.

"We have a proverb that it always snows at Carne in the long nights. That is the traditional term here for the nights of Lent," D'Arcy replied. "Before the Reformation the monks of the Abbey kept a vigil during Lent between the Offices of Compline and Lauds. You may know that already perhaps. As there is no longer a religious order attached to the Abbey, the custom has fallen into disuse. We continue to observe it, however, by the saying of Compline during Lent. Compline was the last of the Canonical Day Hours and was said before retiring for the night. The Master, who has a great respect for traditions of this kind, has reintroduced the old words for our devotions. Prime was the dawn Office, as you are no doubt aware. Terce was at the third hour of daylight—that is to say at 9.0 a.m. Thus we no longer refer to Morning Prayer, but to Terce. I find it delightful. Similarly, during Advent and Lent we say Sext at midday in the Abbey."

"Are all these services compulsory?"

"Of course. Otherwise it would be necessary to make arrangements for those boys who did not attend.

That is not desirable. Besides, you forget that Carne is a religious foundation."

It was a beautiful night. As they crossed the Close, Smiley looked up at the tower. It seemed smaller and more peaceful in the moonlight. The whiteness of the new snow lit the very sky itself; the whole Abbey was so sharply visible against it that even the mutilated images of saints were clear in every sad detail of their deface- ment, wretched figures, their purpose lost, with no eyes to see the changing world.

They reached the cross-roads to the south of the Abbey.

"The parting of the ways, I fear," said D'Arcy, ex- tending his hand.

"It's a beautiful night," Smiley replied quickly, "let me come with you as far as your house."

"Gladly," said D'Arcy drily.

They turned down North Fields Lane. A high stone wall ran along one side; and on the other the great expanse of playing fields, twenty or more rugby pitches, bordered the road for over half a mile. They walked this distance in silence, until D'Arcy stopped and pointed with his stick past Smiley towards a small house on the edge of the playing fields.

"That's North Fields, the Rodes' house. It used to belong to the head groundsman, but the school added a wing a few years ago, and now it's a staff house. My own house is rather larger, and lies further up the road. Happily, I am fond of walking."

"Was it along here that you found Stanley Rode that night?"

There was a pause, then D'Arcy said: "It was nearer to my house, about a quarter of a mile further on. He was in a terrible condition, poor fellow, terrible. I am myself unable to bear the sight of blood. If I had known how he would look when I brought him into the house, I do not think I could have done it. Mercifully, my sister Dorothy is a most competent woman."

They walked on in silence, until Smiley said: "From what you were saying at dinner, the Rodes were a very ill-assorted couple."

"Precisely. If her death had happened any other way, I would describe it as providential: a blessed release for Rode. She was a thoroughly mischievous woman, Smiley, who made it her business to hold her husband up to ridicule. I believe it was intentional. Others do not. I do, and I have my reasons. She took pleasure in deriding her husband."

"And Carne too, no doubt."

"Just so. This is a critical moment in Carne's development. Many Public Schools have conceded to the vulgar clamour for change—change at any price. Carne, I am pleased to say, has not joined these Gadarene swine. That makes it more important than ever that we protect ourselves from within as well as from without." He spoke with surprising vehemence.

"But was she really such a problem? Surely her husband could have spoken to her?"

"I never encouraged him to do so, I assure you. It is not my practice to interfere between man and wife."

They reached D'Arcy's house. A high laurel hedge entirely concealed the house from the road, except for two multiple chimney-stacks which were visible over the top of it, confirming Smiley's impression that the house was large and Victorian.

"I am not ashamed of the Victorian taste," said D'Arcy as he slowly opened the gate; "but then, I am afraid we are not close to the modern idiom at Carne. This house used to be the rectory for North Fields Church, but the church is now served by a priest-in-charge from the Abbey. The vicarage is still within the school's gift, and I was fortunate enough to receive it. Good night. You must come for sherry before you go. Do you stay long?"

"I doubt it," Smiley replied, "but I am sure you have enough worries at the moment."

"What do you mean?" D'Arcy said sharply.

"The press, the police and all the attendant fuss."

"Ah yes, just so. Quite so. Nevertheless, our community life must continue. We always have a small party in the middle of the Half, and I feel it is particularly important that we should do so on this occasion. I

will send a note to the Sawley tomorrow. My sister
would be charmed. Good night." He clanged the gate
to, and the sound was greeted by the frantic barking of
dogs from somewhere behind the house. A window
opened and a harsh female voice called:

"Is that you, Felix?"

"Yes, Dorothy."

"Why do you have to make such a bloody noise?
You've woken those dogs again." The window closed
with a significant thud, and D'Arcy, without so much as
a glance in Smiley's direction, disappeared quickly into
the shadow of the house.

Smiley set off along the road again, back towards
the town. After walking for about ten minutes he
stopped and looked again towards the Rodes' house a
hundred yards across the playing fields. It lay in the
shadow of a small coppice of fir trees, dark and secret
against the white fields. A narrow lane led towards the
house; there was a brick pillar-box on one corner and a
small oak sign-post, quite new, pointed along the lane,
which must, he decided, lead to the village of Pylle. The
legend upon the sign was obscured by a film of snow,
and Smiley brushed it away with his hand, so that he
could read the words "North Fields," done in a contrived suburban Gothic script which must have caused
D'Arcy considerable discomfort. The snow in the lane
was untrodden; obviously more had fallen recently.
There could not be much traffic between Pylle and
Carne. Glancing quickly up and down the main road he
began making his way along the lane. The hedge rose
high on either side, and soon Smiley could see nothing
but the pale sky above him, and the straggling willow
wands reaching towards it. Once he thought he heard
the sound of a footstep close behind him, but when he
stopped he heard nothing but the furtive rustle of the
laden hedges. He grew more conscious of the cold: it
seemed to hang in the still damp of the sunken road, to
clutch and hold him like the chill air of an empty house.
Soon the hedge on his left gave way to a sparse line of
trees, which Smiley judged to belong to the coppice he

had seen from the road. The snow beneath the trees was patchy, and the bare ground looked suddenly ugly and torn. The lane took him in a gradual curve to the left and, quite suddenly the house stood before him, gaunt and craggy in the moonlight. The walls were brick and flint, half obscured by the mass of ivy which grew in profusion across them, tumbling over the porch in a tangled mane.

He glanced towards the garden. The coppice which bordered the lane encroached almost as far as the corner of the house, and extended to the far end of the lawn, screening the house from the playing fields. The murderer had reached the house by a path which led across the lawn and through the trees to the lane at the furthest end of the garden. Looking carefully at the snow on the lawn, he was able to discern the course of the path. The white glazed door to the left of the house must lead to the conservatory . . . And suddenly he knew he was afraid—afraid of the house, afraid of the sprawling dark garden. The knowledge came to him like an awareness of pain. The ivy walls seemed to reach forward and hold him, like an old woman cosseting an unwilling child. The house was large, yet dingy, holding to itself unearthly shapes, black and oily in the sudden contrasts of moonlight. Fascinated despite his fear, he moved towards it. The shadows broke and reformed, darting swiftly and becoming still, hiding in the abundant ivy, or merging with the black windows.

He observed in alarm the first involuntary movement of panic. He was afraid, then suddenly the senses joined in one concerted cry of terror, where sight and sound and touch could no longer be distinguished in the frenzy of his brain. He turned round and ran back to the gate. As he did so, he looked over his shoulder towards the house.

A woman was standing in the path, looking at him, and behind her the conservatory door swung slowly on its hinges.

For a second she stood quite still, then turned and ran back towards the conservatory. Forgetting his fear,

Smiley followed. As he reached the corner of the house he saw to his astonishment that she was standing at the door, rocking it gently back and forth in a thoughtful, leisurely way, like a child. She had her back to Smiley, until suddenly she turned to him and spoke, with a soft Dorset drawl, and the childish lilt of a simpleton:

"I thought you was the Devil, Mister, but you'm got no wings."

Smiley hesitated. If he moved forward, she might take fright again and run. He looked at her across the snow, trying to make her out. She seemed to be wearing a bonnet or shawl over her head, and a dark cape over her shoulders. In her hand she held a sprig of leaves, and these she gently waved back and forth as she spoke to him.

"But you'm carn't do nothin', Mister, 'cos I got the holly fer to hold yer. So you do bide there, Mister, for little Jane can hold yer." She shook the leaves vehemently towards him and began laughing softly. She still had one hand upon the door, and as she spoke her head lolled to one side.

"You bide away from little Jane, Mister, however pretty she'm do be."

"Yes, Jane," said Smiley softly, "you're a very pretty girl, I can see that; and that's a pretty cape you're wearing, Jane."

Evidently pleased with this, she clutched the lapels of her cape and turned slowly round, in a child's parody of a fine lady.

As she turned, Smiley saw the two empty sleeves of an overcoat swinging at her sides.

"There's some do laugh at Janie," she said, a note of petulance in her voice, "but there's not many seen the Devil fly, Mister. But Janie seed 'im, Janie seed 'im. Silver wings like fishes 'e done 'ad, Janie saw."

"Where did you find that coat, Janie?"

She put her hands together and shook her head slowly from side to side.

"He'm a bad one. Ooh, he'm a bad one, Mister," and she laughed softly. "I seed 'im flying, riding on the wind," she laughed again, "and the moon be'ind 'im, lightin' up the way! They'm close as sisters, moon and Devil."

On an impulse Smiley seized a handful of ivy from the side of the house and held it out to her, moving slowly forward as he did so.

"Do you like flowers, Janie? Here are flowers for Janie; pretty flowers for pretty Janie." He had nearly reached her when with remarkable speed she ran across the lawn, disappeared into the trees and ran off down the lane. Smiley let her go. He was drenched in sweat.

As soon as he reached the hotel he telephoned Detective Inspector Rigby.

VII

King Arthur's Church

The coffee lounge of the Sawley Arms resembles nothing so much as the Tropical Plants Pavilion at Kew Gardens. Built in an age when cactus was the most fashionable of plants and bamboo its indispensable companion, the lounge was conceived as the architectural image of a jungle clearing. Steel pillars, fashioned in segments like the trunk of a palm tree, supported a high glass roof whose regal dome replaced the African sky. Enormous urns of bronze or green-glazed earthenware contained all that was elegant and prolific in the cactus world, and between them very old residents could relax on sofas of spindly bamboo, sipping warm coffee and re-living the discomforts of safari.

Smiley's efforts to obtain a bottle of whisky and a syphon of soda at half past eleven at night were not immediately rewarded. It seemed that, like carrion from the carcass, the journalists had gone. The only sign of life in the hotel was the night porter, who treated his request with remote disapproval and advised him to go to bed. Smiley, by no means naturally persistent, discovered a half-crown in his overcoat pocket and thrust it a little irritably into the old man's hand. The result, though not magical, was effective, and by the time Rigby had made his way to the hotel, Smiley was seated

61

in front of a bright gas fire in the coffee lounge with glasses and a whisky bottle before him.

Smiley retold his experiences of the evening with careful accuracy.

"It was the coat that caught my eye. It was a heavy overcoat like a man's," he concluded. "I remembered the blue belt and . . ." He left the sentence unfinished. Rigby nodded, got up and walked briskly across the lounge and through the swing doors to the porter's desk. Ten minutes later, he returned.

"I think we'd better go and pull her in," he said simply. "I've sent for a car."

"We?" asked Smiley.

"Yes, if you wouldn't mind. What's the matter? Are you frightened?"

"Yes," he replied. "Yes, I am."

The village of Pylle lies to the south of North Fields, upon a high spur which rises steeply from the flat, damp pastures of the Carne valley. It consists of a handful of stone cottages and a small inn where you may drink beer in the landlord's parlour. Seen from Carne playing fields, the village could easily be mistaken for an outcrop of rock upon a tor, for the hill on which it stands appears conical from the northern side. Local historians claim that Pylle is the oldest settlement in Dorset, that its name is Anglo-Saxon for harbour, and that it served the Romans as a port when all the lowlands around were covered by the sea. They will tell you, too, that King Arthur rested there after seven months at sea, and paid homage to Saint Andrew, the patron saint of sailors, on the site of Pylle Church, where he burned a candle for each month he had spent afloat; and that in the church, built to commemorate his visit and standing to this day lonely and untended on the hillside, there is a bronze coin as witness to his visit—the very one King Arthur gave to the verger before he set sail again for the Isle of Avalon.

Inspector William Rigby, himself a keen local historian, gave Smiley a somewhat terse précis of Pylle's legendary past as he drove cautiously along the snow-covered lanes.

"These small, out-of-the-way villages are pretty strange places," he concluded. "Often only three or four families, all so inbred you can no more sort them out than a barnful of cats. That's where your village idiots come from. They call it the Devil's Mark; I call it incest. They hate to have them in the village, you know—they'll drive them away at any price, like trying to wash away their shame, if you follow me."

"I follow you."

"This Jane's the religious sort. There's one or two of them turn that way. The villagers at Pylle are all Chapel now, see, so there's been no use for King Arthur's Church since Wesley. It's empty, falling to bits. There's a few from the valley go up to see it, for its history, like, but no one cares for it, or didn't not till Janie moved in."

"Moved in?"

"Yes. She's taken to cleaning the church out night and day, bringing in wild flowers and such. That's why they say she's a witch."

They passed Rode's house in silence and after turning a sharp bend began climbing the long steep hill that led to Pylle village. The snow in the lane was untouched and apart from occasional skidding they progressed without difficulty. The lower slopes of the hill were wooded, and the lane dark, until suddenly they emerged to find themselves on a smooth plateau, where a savage wind blew the fine snow like smoke across the fields, whipping it against the car. The snow had risen in drifts to one side of the lane, and the going became increasingly difficult.

Finally Rigby stopped the car and said:

"We'll walk from here, sir, if you don't mind."

"How far is it?"

"Short and sour, I'd say. That's the village straight ahead."

Through the windscreen, Smiley could discern behind the drifting veils of blown snow two low buildings about a quarter of a mile away. As he looked, a tall, muffled figure advanced towards them along the lane.

"That's Ted Mundy," said Rigby with satisfaction, "I told him to be here. He's the sergeant from Okeford." He leaned out of the car window and called merrily:

"Hullo, Ted there, you old buzzard, how be?" Rigby opened the back door of the car and the sergeant climbed in. Smiley and Mundy were briefly introduced.

"There's a light in the church," said Mundy, "but I don't know whether Janie's there. I can't ask no one in the village, see, or I'd have the whole lot round me. They thought she'd gone for good."

"Does she sleep there then, Ted? She got a bed there or something?" Rigby asked, and Smiley noticed with pleasure that his Dorset accent was more pronounced when he spoke to Mundy.

"So they say, Bill. I couldn't find no bed when I looked in there Saturday. But I tell you an odd thing, Bill. It seems Mrs. Rode used to come up here sometimes, to the chapel, to see Janie."

"I heard about that," said Rigby shortly. "Now which way's the church, Ted?"

"Over the hill," said Mundy. "Outside the village, in a paddock." He turned to Smiley. "That's quite common round here, sir, as I expect you know." Mundy spoke very slowly, choosing his words. "You see, when they had the plague they left their dead in the villages and moved away; not far though, on account of their land and the church. Terrible it was, terrible." Somehow Mundy managed to imply that the Black Death was a fairly recent disaster in those parts, if not actually within living memory.

They got out of the car, forcing the doors against the strong wind, and made their way towards the village, Mundy leading and Smiley in third place. The driven snow, fine and hard, stung their faces. It was an unearthly walk, high on that white hill on such a night. The curve of the bleak hill's crest and the moaning of the wind, the snow cloud which sped across the moon,

the dismal, unlit cottages so cautiously passed, belonged
to another corner of the world.

Mundy led them sharply to the left, and Smiley
guessed that by avoiding the centre of the village he
hoped to escape the notice of its inhabitants. After
about twenty minutes' walking, often through deep
snow, they found themselves following a low hedge between two fields. In the furthest corner of the right
hand field they saw a pale light glimmering across the
snow, so pale that at first Smiley had to look away from
it, then run his eyes back along the line of that distant
hedge to make sure he was not deceived. Rigby
stopped, beckoning to the others.

"I'll take over now," he said. He turned to Smiley.
"I'd be obliged, sir, if you'd stand off a little. If there's
any trouble we don't want you mixed up in it, do we?"

"Of course."

"Ted Mundy, you come up by me."

They followed the hedge until they came to a stile.
Through the gap in the hedge they saw the church
clearly now, a low building more like a tithe barn than a
church. At one end a pale glow, like the uncertain light
of a candle, shone dimly through the leaded windows.

"She's there," said Mundy, under his breath, as he
and Rigby moved forward, Smiley following some distance behind.

They were crossing the field now, Rigby leading,
and the church drawing ever closer. New sounds dis-
turbed the moaning of the storm; the parched creak of a
door, the mutter of a crumbling roof, the incessant sigh
of wind upon a dying house. The two men in front of
Smiley had stopped, almost in the shadow of the church
wall, and were whispering together. Then Mundy
walked quietly away, disappearing round the corner of
the church. Rigby waited a moment, then approached
the narrow entrance in the rear wall, and pushed the
door.

It opened slowly, creaking painfully on its hinges.
Then he disappeared into the church. Smiley was waiting outside when suddenly above all the sounds of night

he heard a scream, so taut and shrill and clear that it seemed to have no source, but to ride everywhere upon the wind, to mount the ravaged sky on wings; and Smiley had a vision of Mad Janie as he had seen her earlier that night, and he heard again in her demented cry the dreadful note of madness. For a moment he waited. The echo died. Then slowly, terrified, he walked through the snow to the open doorway.

Two candles and an oil lamp on the bare altar shed a dim light over the tiny chapel. In front of the altar, on the sanctuary step, sat Jane, looking vaguely towards them. Her vacuous face was daubed with stains of green and blue, her filthy clothes were threaded with sprigs of evergreen and all about her on the floor were the bodies of small animals and birds.

The pews were similarly decorated with dead creatures of all kinds; and on the altar, broken twigs and little heaps of holly leaves. Between the candles stood a crudely-fashioned cross. Stepping forward past Rigby, Smiley walked quickly down the aisle, past the lolling figure of Jane, until he stood before the altar. For a moment he hesitated, then turned and called softly to Rigby.

On the cross, draped over its three ends like a crude diadem, was a string of green beads.

VIII

Flowers For Stella

He woke with the echo of her scream in his ears. He had meant to sleep late, but his watch said half past seven. He put on his bedside lamp, for it was still half-dark, and peered owlishly round the room. There were his trousers, flung over the chair, the legs still sodden from the snow. There were his shoes; he'd have to buy another pair. And there beside him were the notes he had made early that morning before going to sleep, transcriptions from memory of some of Mad Jane's monologue on the journey back to Carne, a journey he would never forget. Mundy had sat with her in the back. She spoke to herself as a child does, asking questions and then in the patient tones of an adult for whom the reply is self-evident, providing the answer.

One obsession seemed to fill her mind: she had seen the devil. She had seen him flying on the wind, his silver wings stretched out behind him. Sometimes the recollection amused her, sometimes inflated her with a sense of her own importance or beauty, and sometimes it terrified her, so that she moaned and wept and begged him to go away. Then Mundy would speak kindly to her, and try to calm her. Smiley wondered whether policemen grew accustomed to the squalor of such things, to clothes that were no more than stinking rags wound round wretched limbs, to puling imbeciles

who clutched and screamed and wept. She must have
been living on the run for nights on end, finding her
food in the fields and dustbins since the night of the
murder. . . . What had she done that night? What had
she seen? Had she killed Stella Rode? Had she seen the
murderer, and fancied *him* to be the devil flying on the
wind? Why should she think that? If Janie did not kill
Stella Rode, what had she seen that so frightened her
that for three long winter nights she prowled in terror
like an animal in the forest? Had the devil within taken
hold of Janie and given power to her arm as she struck
down Stella? Was that the devil who rode upon the
wind?

But the beads and the coat and the footprints
which were not hers—what of them? He lay there
thinking, and achieving nothing. At last it was time to
get up: it was the morning of the funeral.

As he was getting out of bed the telephone rang. It
was Rigby. His voice sounded strained and urgent. "I
want to se you," he said. "Can you call round?"

"Before or after the funeral?"

"Before, if possible. What about now?"

"I'll be there in ten minutes."

Rigby looked, for the first time since Smiley had
met him, tired and worried.

"It's Mad Janie," he said. "The Chief thinks we
should charge her."

"What for?"

"Murder," Rigby replied crisply, pushing a thin
file across the table. "The old fool's made a statement
. . . a sort of confession."

They sat in silence while Smiley read the extraordinary statement. It was signed with Mad Janie's
mark—J. L.—drawn in a childish hand in letters an
inch high. The constable who had taken it down had
begun by trying to condense and simplify her account,
but by the end of the first page he had obviously de-
spaired. At last Smiley came to the description of the
murder:

"So I tells my darling, I tells her: 'You are a naughty creature to go with the devil,' but her did not hearken, see, and I took angry with her, but she paid no call. I can't abide them as go with devils in the night, and I told her. She ought to have had holly, mister, there's the truth. I told her, mister, but she never would hearken, and that's all Janie's saying, but she drove the devil off, Janie did, and there's one will thank me, that's my darling and I took her jewels for the saints I did, to pretty out the church, and a coat for to keep me warm."

Rigby watched him as he slowly replaced the statement on the desk.

"Well, what do you think of it?"

Smiley hesitated; "It's pretty good nonsense as it stands," he replied at last.

"Of course it is," said Rigby, with something like contempt. "She saw something, Lord knows what, when she was out on the prowl; stealing, I shouldn't wonder. She may have robbed the body, or else she picked up the beads where the murderer dropped them. We've traced the coat. Belonged to a Mr. Jardine, a baker in Carne East. Mrs. Jardine gave it to Stella Rode last Wednesday morning for the refugees. Janie must have pinched it from the conservatory. That's what she meant by 'a coat for to keep me warm.' But she no more killed Stella Rode than you or I did. What about the footprints, the glove-marks in the conservatory? Besides, she's not strong enough, Janie isn't, to heave that poor woman forty feet through the snow. This is a man's work, as anyone can see."

"Then what exactly . . . ?"

"We've called off the search, and I'm to prepare a case against one Jane Lyn of the village of Pylle for the wilful murder of Stella Rode. I wanted to tell you myself before you read it all over the papers. So that you'd know how it was."

"Thanks."

"In the meantime, if there's any help I can give

you, we're still willing." He hesitated, seemed about to
say something, then to change his mind.

As he made his way down the wide staircase Smiley felt useless and very angry, which was scarcely the
right frame of mind in which to attend a funeral.

It was an admirably conducted affair. Neither the
flowers nor the congregation exceeded what was fitting
to the occasion. She was not buried at the Abbey, out of
deference perhaps to her simplicity of taste, but in the
parish churchyard not far from North Fields. The Master
was detained that day, as he was on most days, and had
sent instead his wife, a small, very vague woman who
had spent a long time in India. D'Arcy was much in
evidence, fluttering here and there before the ceremony
like an anxious beadle; and Mr. Cardew had come to
guide poor Stella through the unfamiliarities of High
Anglican procedure. The Hechts were there, Charles all
in black, scrubbed and shining, and Shane in dramatic
weeds, and a hat with a very broad brim.

Smiley, who, like the others, had arrived early in
anticipation of the unwholesome public interest which
the ceremony might arouse, found himself a seat near
the entrance of the church. He watched each new ar-
rival with interest, waiting for his first sight of Stanley
Rode.

Several tradesmen arrived, pressed into bulging
serge and black ties, and formed a small group south of
the aisle, away from the staff and their wives. Soon they
were joined by other members of the town community,
women who had known Mrs. Rode at the Tabernacle;
and then by Rigby, who looked straight at Smiley and
gave no sign. Then on the stroke of three a tall old man
walked slowly through the doorway, looking straight before him, neither knowing nor seeing anyone. Beside
him was Stanley Rode.

It was a face which at first sight meant nothing to
Smiley, seeming to have neither the imprint of temperament nor the components of character; it was a shallow,
ordinary face, inclining to plumpness, and lacking quality. It matched his short, ordinary body and his black,

ordinary hair; it was suitably compressed into an expression of sorrow. As Smiley watched him turn into the centre aisle and take his place among the principal mourners, it occurred to him that Rode's very walk and bearing successfully conveyed something entirely alien to Carne. If it is vulgar to wear a pen in the breast pocket of your jacket, to favour Fair Isle pullovers and brown ties, to bob a little and turn your feet out as you walk, then Rode beyond a shadow of doubt was vulgar, for though he did not now commit these sins, his manner implied them all.

They followed the coffin into the churchyard and gathered round the open grave. D'Arcy and Fielding were standing together, seemingly intent upon the service. The tall, elderly figure who had entered the church with Rode was now visibly moved, and Smiley guessed that he was Stella's father, Samuel Glaston. As the service ended, the old man walked quickly away from the crowd, nodding briefly to Rode, and disappeared into the church. He seemed to struggle as he went, like a man walking against a strong wind.

The little group moved slowly away from the graveside, until only Rode remained, an oddly stiff figure, taut and constrained, his eyes wide but somehow sightless, his mouth set in a strict, pedagogic line. Then, as Smiley watched, Rode seemed to wake from a dream; his body suddenly relaxed and he too walked slowly but quite confidently away from the grave towards the small group which by now had reassembled at the churchyard gate. As he did so, Fielding, at the edge of the group, caught sight of him approaching and, to Smiley's astonishment, walked deliberately and quite quickly away with an expression of strong distaste. It was not the calculated act of a man wishing to insult another, for it attracted the notice neither of Rode nor of anyone else standing by. Terence Fielding, for once, appeared to be in the grip of a genuine emotion, and indifferent to the impression he created.

Reluctantly Smiley approached the group. Rode was rather to one side, the D'Arcys were there, and three or four members of the staff. No one was talking much.

"Mr. Rode?" he enquired.

"That's right, yes." He spoke slowly, a trace of an accent carefully avoided.

"I'm representing Miss Brimley of the *Christian Voice*."

"Oh, yes."

"She was most anxious that the journal should be represented. I thought you would like to know that."

"I saw your wreath; very kind, I am sure."

"Your wife was one of our most loyal supporters," Smiley continued. "We regarded her almost as one of the family."

"Yes, she was very keen on the *Voice*." Smiley wondered whether Rode was always as impassive as this, or whether bereavement had made him listless.

"When did you come?" Rode asked suddenly.

"On Friday."

"Making a week-end of it, eh?"

Smiley was so astonished that for a moment he could think of nothing to say. Rode was still looking at him, waiting for an answer.

"I have one or two friends here . . . Mr. Fielding. . . ."

"Oh, Terence." Smiley was convinced that Rode was not on Christian-name terms with Fielding.

"I would like, if I may," Smiley ventured, "to write a small obituary for Miss Brimley. Would you have any objection?"

"Stella would have liked that."

"If you are not too upset, perhaps I could call round tomorrow for one or two details?"

"Certainly."

"Eleven o'clock?"

"It will be a pleasure," Rode replied, almost pertly, and they walked together to the churchyard gate.

IX

The Mourners

It was a cheap trick to play on a man who had suddenly
lost his wife. Smiley knew that. As he gently unlatched
the gate and entered the drive, where two nights ago he
had conducted his strange conversation with Jane Lyn,
he acknowledged that in calling on Rode under any pre-
text at such a time he was committing a thoroughly un-
principled act. It was a peculiarity of Smiley's character
that throughout the whole of his clandestine work he
had never managed to reconcile the means to the end.
A stringent critic of his own motives, he had discovered
after long observation that he tended to be less a creature of intellect than his tastes and habits might suggest;
once in the war he had been described by his superiors
as possessing the cunning of Satan and the conscience
of a virgin, which seemed to him not wholly unjust.

He pressed the bell and waited.

Stanley Rode opened the door. He was very neatly
dressed, very scrubbed.

"Oh hullo," he said, as if they were old friends. "I
say, you haven't got a car, have you?"

"I'm afraid I left it in London."

"Never mind." Rode sounded disappointed.
"Thought we might have gone out for a drive, had a
chat as we went. I get a bit fed-up, kicking around here
on my own. Miss D'Arcy asked me to stay over at their

73

place. Very good people they are, very good indeed; but somehow I didn't wish it, not yet."

"I understand."

"Do you?" They were in the hall now, Smiley was getting out of his overcoat, Rode waiting to receive it. "I don't think many do—the loneliness I mean. Do you know what they've done, the Master and Mr. D'Arcy? They meant it well, I know. They've farmed out all my correcting—my exam. correcting, you understand. What am I supposed to do here, all on my own? I've no teaching, nothing; they've all taken a hand. You'd think they wanted to get rid of me."

Smiley nodded vaguely. They moved towards the drawing-room, Rode leading the way.

"I know they did it for the best, as I said. But after all, I've got to spend the time somehow. Simon Snow got some of my division to correct. Have you met him by any chance? Sixty-one per cent. He gave one boy—sixty-one. The boy's an absolute fool; I told Fielding at the beginning of the Half that he wouldn't possibly get his Remove. Perkins his name is, a nice enough boy; head of Fielding's house. He'd have been lucky to get thirty per cent. . . . sixty-one, Snow gave him. I haven't seen the papers yet, of course, but it's impossible, quite impossible."

They sat down.

"Not that I don't want the boy to get on. He's a nice enough boy, nothing special, but well-mannered. Mrs. Rode and I meant to have him here to tea this Half. We would have, in fact, if it hadn't been for . . ." There was a moment's silence. Smiley was going to speak when Rode stood up and said:

"I've a kettle on the stove, Mr. . . . ."

"Smiley."

"I've a kettle on the stove, Mr. Smiley. May I make you a cup of coffee?" That little stiff voice with the corners carefully defined, like a hired morning suit, thought Smiley.

Rode returned a few minutes later with a tray and measured their coffee in precise quantities, according to their taste.

Smiley found himself continually irritated by Rode's social assumptions, and his constant struggle to conceal his origin. You could tell all the time, from every word and gesture, what he was; from the angle of his elbow as he drank his coffee, from the swift, expert pluck at the knee of his trouser leg as he sat down.

"I wonder," Smiley began, "whether perhaps I might now . . ."

"Go ahead, Mr. Smiley."

"We are, of course, largely interested in Mrs. Rode's association with . . . our Church."

"Quite."

"You were married at Branxome, I believe."

"Branxome Hill Tabernacle; fine church." D'Arcy wouldn't have liked the way he said that; cocksure lad on a motor-bike. Pencils in the outside pocket.

"When was that?"

"September, fifty-one."

"Did Mrs. Rode engage in charitable work in Branxome? I know she was very active here."

"No, not at Branxome, but a lot here. She had to look after her father at Branxome, you see. It was refugee relief she was keen on here. That didn't get going much until late 1956—the Hungarians began it, and then this last year. . . ."

Smiley peered thoughtfully at Rode from behind his spectacles, forgot himself, blinked, and looked away.

"Did she take a large part in the social activities of Carne? Does the staff have its own Women's Institute and so on?" he asked innocently.

"She did a bit, yes. But, being Chapel, she kept mainly with the Chapel people from the town . . . you should ask Mr. Cardew about that; he's the Minister."

"But may I say, Mr. Rode, that she took an active part in school affairs as well?"

Rode hesitated.

"Yes, of course," he said.

"Thank you."

There was a moment's silence, then Smiley continued: "Our readers will, of course, remember Mrs. Rode

as the winner of our Kitchen Hints competition. Was
she a good cook, Mr. Rode?"

"Very good, for plain things, not fancy."

"Is there any little fact that you would specially
like us to include, anything she herself would like to be
remembered by?"

Rode looked at him with expressionless eyes. Then
he shrugged.

"No, not really. I can't think of anything. Oh, you
could say her father was a magistrate up North. She was
proud of that."

Smiley finished his coffee and stood up.

"You've been very patient with me, Mr. Rode.
We're most grateful, I assure you. I'll take care to send
you an advance copy of our notice. . . ."

"Thanks. I did it for her, you see. She liked the
Voice; always did. Grew up with it."

They shook hands.

"By the way, do you know where I can find old
Mr. Glaston? Is he staying in Carne or has he returned
to Branxome?"

"He was up here yesterday. He's going back to
Branxome this afternoon. The police wanted to see him
before he left."

"I see."

"He's staying at the Sawley."

"Thank you. I might try and see him before I go."

"When do you leave, then?"

"Quite soon, I expect. Goodbye, then, Mr. Rode.
Incidentally——" Smiley began.

"Yes?"

"If ever you're in London and at a loose end, if
ever you want a chat . . . and a cup of tea, we're always pleased to see you at the *Voice*, you know. Always."

"Thanks. Thanks very much Mr.——"

"Smiley."

"Thanks, that's very decent. No one's said that to
me for a long time. I'll take you up on that one day.
Very good of you."

"Goodbye." Again they shook hands; Rode's was dry and cool. Smooth.

He returned to the Sawley Arms, sat himself at a desk in the empty residents' lounge and wrote a note to Mr. Glaston:

> Dear Mr. Glaston,
>   I am here on behalf of Miss Brimley of the Christian Voice. I have some letters from Stella which I think you would like to see. Forgive me for bothering you at this sad moment; I understand you are leaving Carne this afternoon and wondered if I might see you before you left.

He carefully sealed the envelope and took it to the reception desk. There was no one there, so he rang the bell and waited. At last a porter came, an old turnkey with a grey, bristly face, and after examining the envelope critically for a long time, he agreed, against an excessive fee, to convey it to Mr. Glaston's room. Smiley stayed at the desk, waiting for his answer.

Smiley himself was one of those solitaries who seem to have come into the world fully educated at the age of eighteen. Obscurity was his nature, as well as his profession. The byways of espionage are not populated by the brash and colourful adventurers of fiction. A man who, like Smiley, has lived and worked for years among his country's enemies learns only one prayer: that he may never, never be noticed. Assimilation is his highest aim, he learns to love the crowds who pass him in the street without a glance; he clings to them for his anonymity and his safety. His fear makes him servile—he could embrace the shoppers who jostle him in their impatience, and force him from the pavement. He could adore the officials, the police, the bus conductors, for the terse indifference of their attitudes.

But this fear, this servility, this dependence, had developed in Smiley a perception for the colour of human beings: a swift, feminine sensitivity to their characters and motives. He knew mankind as a huntsman

knows his cover, as a fox the wood. For a spy must
hunt while he is hunted, and the crowd is his estate. He
could collect their gestures and their words, record the
interplay of glance and movement, as a huntsman can
record the twisted bracken and the broken twig, or as a
fox detects the signs of danger.

Thus, while he waited patiently for Glaston's reply
and recalled the crowded events of the last forty-eight
hours, he was able to order and assess them with de-
tachment. What was the cause of D'Arcy's attitude to
Fielding, as if they were unwilling partners to a shabby
secret? Staring across the neglected hotel gardens towards Carne Abbey, he was able to glimpse behind the
lead roof of the Abbey the familiar battlements of the
school: keeping the new world out and the old world
secure. In his mind's eye he saw the Great Court now,
as the boys came out of Chapel: the black-coated
groups in the leisured attitudes of eighteenth-century
England. And he remembered the other school beside
the police station: Carne High School; a little tawdry
place like a porter's lodge in an empty graveyard, as
detached from the tones of Carne as its brick and flint
from the saffron battlements of School Hall.

Yes, he reflected, Stanley Rode had made a long,
long journey from the grammar school at Branxome.
And if he killed his wife, then the motive, Smiley was
sure, and even the means, were to be found in that hard
road to Carne.

"It was kind of you to come," said Glaston; "kind
of Miss Brimley to send you. They're good people at
the *Voice*; always were." He said this as if "good" were
an absolute quality with which he was familiar.

"You'd better read the letters, Mr. Glaston. The
second one will shock you, I'm afraid, but I'm sure
you'll agree that it would be wrong of me not to show it
to you." They were sitting in the lounge, the mammoth
plants like sentinels beside them.

He handed Glaston the two letters, and the old
man took them firmly and read them. He held them a
good way from him to read, thrusting his strong head

back, his eyes half closed, the crisp line of his mouth turned down at the corners. At last he said:

"You were with Miss Brimley in the war, were you?"

"I worked with John Landsbury, yes."

"I see. That's why she came to you?"

"Yes."

"Are you Chapel?"

"No."

He was silent for a while, his hands folded on his lap, the letters before him on the table.

"Stanley was Chapel when they married. Then he went over. Did you know that?"

"Yes."

"Where I come from in the North, we don't do that. Chapel was something we'd stood up for and won. Almost like the vote."

"I know."

His back was as straight as a soldier's. He looked stern rather than sad. Quite suddenly, his eyes turned towards Smiley, and he looked at him long and carefully.

"Are you a schoolmaster?" he asked, and it occurred to Smiley that in his day Samuel Glaston had been a very shrewd man of business.

"No. . . . I'm more or less retired."

"Married?"

"I was."

Again the old man fell silent, and Smiley wished he had left him alone.

"She was a great one for chatter," he said at last. Smiley said nothing.

"Have you told the police?"

"Yes, but they knew already. That is, they knew that Stella thought her husband was going to murder her. She'd tried to tell Mr. Cardew. . . ."

"The Minister?"

"Yes. He thought she was overwrought and . . . deluded."

"Do you think she wasn't?"

"I don't know. I just don't know. But from what I

have heard of your daughter I don't believe she was unbalanced. *Something* roused her suspicions, something
frightened her very much. I don't believe we can just
disregard that. I don't believe it was a coincidence that
she was frightened before she died. And therefore I
don't believe that the beggar-woman murdered her."

Samuel Glaston nodded slowly. It seemed to Smiley that the old man was trying to show interest, partly
to be polite, and partly because if he did not it would be
a confession that he had lost interest in life itself.

Then, after a long silence, he carefully folded up
the letters and gave them back. Smiley waited for him
to speak, but he said nothing.

After a few moments Smiley got up and walked
quietly from the room.

X

Little Women

Shane Hecht smiled, and drank some more sherry. "You must be dreadfully important," she said to Smiley, "for D'Arcy to serve decent sherry. What are you, *Almanach de Gotha*?"

"I'm afraid not. D'Arcy and I were both dining at Terence Fielding's on Saturday night and D'Arcy asked me for sherry."

"Terence is *wicked*, isn't he? Charles loathes him. I'm afraid they see Sparta in *quite* different ways. . . . Poor Terence. It's his last Half, you know."

"I know."

"So sweet of you to come to the funeral yesterday. I hate funerals, don't you? Black is so insanitary. I always remember King George V's funeral. Lord Sawley was at Court in those days, and gave Charles two tickets. So kind. I always think it's *spoilt* us for ordinary funerals in a way. Although I'm never quite *sure* about funerals, are you? I have a suspicion that they are largely a lower-class recreation; cherry brandy and seed cake in the parlour. I think the tendency of people like ourselves is for a *quiet* funeral these days; no flowers, just a short obituary and a memorial service later." Her small eyes were bright with pleasure. She finished her sherry and held out her empty glass to Smiley.

"Would you mind, dear. I hate sherry, but Felix is so mean."

Smiley filled her glass from the decanter on the table.

"Dreadful about the murder, wasn't it? That beggar-woman must be mad. Stella Rode was such a nice person, I always thought . . . and so *unusual*. She did such clever things with the same dress. . . . But she had such curious friends. All for Hans the woodcutter and Pedro the fisherman, if you know what I mean."

"Was she popular at Carne?"

Shane Hecht laughed gently: "No one is popular at Carne . . . but she wasn't easy to like. . . . She would wear black crêpe on Sundays. . . . Forgive me, but do the lower classes always do that? The townspeople liked her, I believe. They adore anyone who betrays Carne. But then she was a Christian Scientist or something."

"Baptist, I understand," said Smiley unthinkingly.

She looked at him for a moment with unfeigned curiosity. "How sweet," she murmured. "Tell me, what *are* you?"

Smiley made some facetious reply about being unemployed, and realised that it was only by a hair's-breadth that he had avoided explaining himself to Shane Hecht like a small boy. Her very ugliness, her size and voice, coupled with the sophisticated malice of her conversation, gave her the dangerous quality of command. Smiley was tempted to compare her with Fielding, but for Fielding other people scarcely existed. For Shane Hecht they did exist: they were there to be found wanting in the minute tests of social behaviour, to be ridiculed, cut off and destroyed.

"I read in the paper that her father was quite well off. From the North. Second generation. Remarkable really how *unspoilt* she was . . . so natural. . . . You wouldn't think she *needed* to go to the launderette or to make friends with beggars. . . . Though, of course, the Midlands are different, aren't they? Only about three good families between Ipswich and Newcastle. Where did you say you came from, dear?"

"London."

"How nice. I went to tea with Stella once. Milk in first and Indian. So different," and she looked at Smiley suddenly and said "I'll tell you something. She almost aroused an admiration in me, I found her so insufferable. She was one of those tiresome little snobs who think that only the humble are virtuous." Then she smiled and added, "I even agreed with Charles about Stella Rode, and that's saying something. If you're a student of mankind, do go and have a look at him, the contrast is riveting." But at that moment they were joined by D'Arcy's sister, a bony, virile woman with untidy grey hair and an arrogant, hunting mouth.

"Dorothy darling," Shane murmured; "such a lovely party. So *kind*. And so *exciting* to meet somebody from London, don't you think? We were talking about poor Mrs. Rode's funeral."

"Stella Rode may have been damn' bad form, Shane, but she did a lot for my refugees."

"Refugees?" asked Smiley innocently.

"Hungarians. Collecting for them. Clothes, furniture, money. One of the few wives who *did* anything." She looked sharply at Shane Hecht, who was smiling benignly past her towards her husband: "Busy little creature, she was; didn't mind rolling her sleeves up, going from door to door. Got her little women on to it at the Baptist chapel and brought in a mass of stuff. You've got to hand it to them, you know. They've got *spirit*. Felix, more sherry!"

There were about twenty in the two rooms, but Smiley, who had arrived a little late, found himself attached to a group of about eight who stood nearest the door: D'Arcy and his sister; Charles and Shane Hecht; a young mathematician called Snow and his wife; a curate from the Abbey and Smiley himself, bewildered and mole-like behind his spectacles. Smiley looked quickly round the room, but could see no sign of Fielding.

". . . Yes," Dorothy D'Arcy continued, "she was a good little worker, very . . . right to the end. I went over there on Friday with that parson man from the tin tabernacle—Cardew—to see if there was any refugee

stuff to tidy up. There wasn't a thing out of place—
every bit of clothing she had was all packed up and addressed; we just had to send it off. She was a damn'
good little worker, I will say. Did a splendid job at the
bazaar, you know."

"Yes, darling," said Shane Hecht sweetly. "I remember it well. It was the day I presented her to lady
Sawley. She wore such a *nice* little hat—the one she
wore on Sundays, you know. And *so* respectful. She
called her 'my lady'." She turned to Smiley and
breathed: "Rather feudal, don't you think, dear? I always like that: so few of us left."

The mathematician and his wife were talking to
Charles Hecht in a corner and a few minutes later Smiley managed to extricate himself from the group and join
them.

Ann Snow was a pretty girl with a rather square
face and a turned-up nose. Her husband was tall and
thin, with an agreeable stoop. He held his sherry glass
between straight, slender fingers as if it were a chemical
retort and when he spoke he seemed to address the
sherry rather than his listener; Smiley remembered them
from the funeral. Hecht was looking pink and rather
cross, sucking at his pipe. They talked in a desultory
way, their conversation dwarfed by the exchanges of the
adjoining group. Hecht eventually drifted away from
them, still frowning and withdrawn, and stood ostenta-
tiously alone near the door.

"Poor Stella," said Ann Snow after a moment's silence. "Sorry," she added. "I can't get her out of my
mind yet. It seems mad, just mad. I mean why should
she *do* it, that Janie woman?"

"Did you like Stella?" Smiley asked.

"Of course we did. She was sweet. We've been
here four Halves now, but she was the only person here
who's ever been *kind* to us." Her husband said nothing,
just nodded at his sherry. "Simon wasn't a boy at
Carne, you see—most of the staff were—so we didn't
know anyone and no one was really interested. They all
pretended to be terribly pleased with us, of course, but
it was Stella who really . . ."

Dorothy D'Arcy was descending on them. "Mrs. Snow," she said crisply, "I've been meaning to talk to you. I want you to take over Stella Rode's job on the refugees." She cast an appraising look in Simon's direction: "The Master's very keen on refugees."

"Oh, my goodness!" Ann Snow replied, aghast. "I couldn't possibly, Miss D'Arcy, I . . ."

"Couldn't? Why couldn't you? You helped Mrs. Rode with her stall at the bazaar, didn't you?"

"So that's where she got her clothes from," breathed Shane Hecht behind them. Ann was fumbling on:

"But . . . well I haven't quite got Stella's nerve, if you understand what I mean; and besides, she was a Baptist: all the locals helped her and gave her things, and they all liked her. With me it would be different."

"Lot of damn' nonsense," declared Miss D'Arcy, who spoke to all her juniors as if they were grooms or erring children; and Shane Hecht beside her said: "Baptists are the people who don't like private pews, aren't they? I do so agree—one feels that if one's paid one simply has to go."

The curate who had been talking cricket in a corner, was startled into mild protest: "Oh, come, Mrs. Hecht, the private pew had many advantages . . ." and embarked on a diffuse apologia for ancient custom, to which Shane listened with every sign of the most assiduous interest. When at last he finished she said: "Thank you, William dear, so sweet," turned her back on him and added to Smiley in a stage whisper: "William Trumper—one of Charles' old pupils—such a triumph when he passed his Certificate."

Smiley, anxious to dissociate himself from Shane Hecht's vengeance on the curate, turned to Ann Snow, but she was still at the mercy of Miss D'Arcy's charitable intentions, and Shane was still talking to him:

"The only Smiley I ever heard of married Lady Ann Sercombe at the end of the war. She left him soon afterwards, of course. A very curious match. I understand he was quite unsuitable. She was Lord Sawley's cousin, you know. The Sawleys have been connected with Carne for four hundred years. The present heir is a pupil of Charles; we often dine at the Castle. I never did hear what became of Ann Sercombe . . . she went to Africa, you know . . . or was it India? No it was America. So tragic. One doesn't talk about it at the Castle." For a moment the noise in the room stopped. For a moment, no more, he could discern nothing but the steady gaze of Shane Hecht upon him, and knew she was waiting for an answer. And then she released him as if to say: "I could crush you, you see. But I won't, I'll let you live," and she turned and walked away.

He contrived to take his leave at the same time as Ann and Simon Snow. They had an old car and insisted on running Smiley back to his hotel. On the way there, he said:

"If you have nothing better to do, I would be happy to give you both dinner at my hotel. I imagine the food is dreadful."

The Snows protested and accepted, and a quarter of an hour later they were all three seated in a corner of the enormous dining-room of the Sawley Arms, to the great despondency of three waiters and a dozen generations of Lord Sawley's forbears, puffy men in crumbling pigment.

"We really got to know her our second Half," Ann Snow ran on. "Stella didn't do much mixing with the other wives—she'd learnt her lesson by then. She didn't go to coffee parties and things, so it was really luck that we did meet. When we first came there wasn't a staff house available for us: we had to spend the first Half in a hotel. We moved in to a little house in Bread Street at the end of our second Half. Moving was chaos—Simon was examining for the scholarships and we were terribly broke, so we had to do everything we possibly could for ourselves. It was a wet Thursday morning when we moved. The rain was simply teeming down; but none of our good pieces would get in through the front door, and in the end Mulligan's just dumped me on the doorstep and let me sort it out." She laughed, and Smiley thought what an agreeable child she was. "They were absolutely foul. They would have just driven off, I think, but they wanted a cheque as soon as they'd done the delivery, and the bill was pounds more than the estimate. I hadn't got the cheque-book, of course. Simon had gone off with it. Mulligan's even threatened to take all the stuff away again. It was monstrous. I think I was nearly in tears." She nearly is now, thought Smiley. "Then out of the blue Stella turned up. I can't think how she even knew we were moving—I'm sure no one else did. She'd brought an overall and an old pair of shoes and she'd come to help. When she saw what was going on she didn't bother with the men at all, just went to a phone and rang Mr. Mulligan himself. I don't know what she said to him, but she made the foreman talk to him afterwards and there was no more trouble after that. She was terribly happy—happy to *help*. She was that sort of person. They took the door right out and managed to get everything in. She was marvellous at helping without managing. The rest of the wives," she added bitterly, "are awfully good at managing, but don't help at all."

Smiley nodded, and discreetly filled their glasses.

"Simon's leaving," Ann said, suddenly confidential. "He's got a grant and we're going back to Oxford. He's going to do a D.Phil. and get a University job."

They drank to his success, and the conversation turned to other things until Smiley asked: "What's Rode himself like to work with?"

"He's a good schoolmaster," said Simon, slowly, "but tiring as a colleague."

"Oh, he was *quite* different from Stella," said Ann. "Terribly Carne-minded. D'Arcy adopted him and he got the bug. Simon says all the grammar school people go that way—it's the fury of the convert. It's sickening. He even changed his religion when he got to Carne. Stella didn't, though; she wouldn't dream of it."

"The Established Church has much to offer at Carne," Simon observed, and Smiley enjoyed the dry precision of his delivery.

"Stella can't exactly have hit it off with Shane Hecht," Smiley probed gently.

"Of *course* she didn't!" Ann declared angrily. "Shane was horrid to her, always sneering at her because she was honest and simple about the things she liked. Shane hated Stella—I think it was because Stella didn't *want* to be a lady of quality. She was quite happy to be herself. That's what really worried Shane. Shane likes people to compete so that she can make fools of them."

"So does Carne," said Simon, quietly.

"She was awfully good at helping out with the refugees. That was how she got into real trouble." Ann Snow's slim hands gently rocked her brandy glass.

"Trouble?"

"Just before she died. Hasn't anyone told you? About her frightful row with D'Arcy's sister?"

"No."

"Of course, they wouldn't have done. Stella never gossiped."

"Let me tell you," said Simon. "It's a good story. When the Refugee Year business started, Dorothy D'Arcy was fired with charitable enthusiasm. So was the Master. Dorothy's enthusiasms always seem to correspond with his. She started collecting clothes and money and packing them off to London. All very laudable, but there was a perfectly good town appeal going, launched by the Mayor. That wasn't good enough for Dorothy, though: the school must have its own appeal; you can't mix your charity. I think Felix was largely behind it. Anyway, after the thing had been going for a few months the refugee centre in London apparently wrote to Dorothy and asked whether anyone would be prepared to accommodate a refugee couple. Instead of publicising the letter, Dorothy wrote straight back and said she would put them up herself. So far so good. The couple turned up, Dorothy and Felix pointed a proud finger at them and the local press wrote it all up as an example of British humanity.

"About six weeks later, one afternoon, these two turned up on Stella's doorstep. The Rodes and the D'Arcys are neighbours, you see, and anyway Stella had tried to take an interest in Dorothy's refugees. The woman was in floods of tears and the husband was shouting blue murder, but that didn't worry Stella. She had them straight into the drawing-room and gave them a cup of tea. Finally, they managed to explain in basic English that they had run away from the D'Arcy's because of the treatment they received. The girl was expected to work from morning till night in the kitchen, and the husband was acting as unpaid kennel-boy for those beastly spaniels that Dorothy breeds. The ones without noses."

"King Charles," Ann prompted.

"It was about as awful as it could be. The girl was pregnant and he was a fully qualified engineer, so neither of them were exactly suited to domestic service. They told Stella that Dorothy was away till the evening—she'd gone to a dog show. Stella advised them to stay with her for the time being, and that evening she went round and told Dorothy what had happened. She had quite a nerve, you see. Although it wasn't nerve really. She just did the simple thing. Dorothy was furious, and demanded that Stella should return 'her refugees' immediately. Stella replied that she was sure that they wouldn't come, and went home. When Stella got home she rang up the refugee people in London and asked their advice. They sent a woman down to see Dorothy and the couple, and the result was that they returned to London the following day. . . . You can imagine what Shane Hecht would have made of that story."

"Didn't she ever find out?"

"Stella never told anyone except us, and we didn't pass it on. Dorothy just let it be known that the refugees had gone to some job in London, and that was that."

"How long ago did this happen?"

"They left exactly three weeks ago," said Ann to her husband. "Stella told me about it when she came to supper the night you were in Oxford for your interview. That was three weeks ago tonight." She turned to Smiley:

"Poor Simon's been having an awful time. Felix

D'Arcy unloaded all Rode's exam. correcting on to him.
It's bad enough doing one person's correction—two is
frantic."

"Yes," replied Simon reflectively. "It's been a bad
week. And rather humiliating in a way. Several of the
boys who were up to me for science last Half are now in
Rode's forms. I'd regarded one or two of them as prac-
tically unteachable, but Rode seems to have brought
them on marvellously. I corrected one boy's paper—
Perkins—sixty-one per cent for elementary science.
Last Half he got fifteen per cent in a much easier paper.
He only got his Remove because Fielding raised hell.
He was in Fielding's house."

"Oh I know—a red-haired boy, a prefect."

"Good Lord," cried Simon. "Don't say you know
him?"

"Oh, Fielding introduced us," said Smiley vaguely.
"Incidentally—no one else ever mentioned that incident
to you about Miss D'Arcy's refugees, did they? Confirmed it, as it were?"

Ann Snow looked at him oddly. "No. Stella told us
about it, but of course Dorothy D'Arcy never referred
to it at all. She must have *hated* Stella, though."

He saw them to their car, and waited despite their
protests while Simon cranked it. At last they drove off,
the car bellowing down the silent street. Smiley stood
for a moment on the pavement, an odd, lonely figure
peering down the empty road.

XI

A Coat To Keep Her Warm

A dog that had not bitten the postman; a devil that rode upon the wind; a woman who knew that she would die; a little, worried man in an overcoat standing in the snow outside his hotel and the laborious chime of the Abbey clock telling him to go to bed.

Smiley hesitated, then with a shrug crossed to the hotel entrance, mounted the step and entered the cheap, yellow light of the residents' hall. He walked slowly up the stairs.

He detested the Sawley Arms. That muted light in the hall was typical: inefficient, antiquated and smug. Like the waiters in the dining-room and the lowered voices in the residents' lounge, like his own hateful bedroom with its blue and gilt urns, and the framed tapestry of a Buckinghamshire garden.

His room was bitterly cold; the maid must have opened the window. He put a shilling in the meter and lit the gas. The fire bubbled grumpily and went out. Muttering, Smiley looked around for some paper to write on, and discovered some, much to his surprise, in the drawer of the writing desk. He changed into his pyjamas and dressing gown and crawled miserably into bed. After sitting there uncomfortably for some minutes he got up, fetched his overcoat and spread it over the eiderdown. A coat for to keep her warm. . . .

How did her statement read? "There's one will thank me, that's my darling and I took her jewels for the saints I did, and a coat for to keep me warm. . . ." The coat had been given to Stella last Wednesday for the refugees. It seemed reasonable to assume from the way the statement read that Janie had taken the coat from the outhouse at the same time as she took the beads from Stella's body. But Dorothy D'Arcy had been round there on Friday morning—of course she had, with Mr. Cardew—she was talking about it at her party that very evening: "There wasn't a thing out of place—every bit of clothing she had was all packed up and addressed—a damn' good little worker, I will say. . . ." Then why hadn't Stella packed the overcoat? If she packed everything else, why not the overcoat too?

Or had Janie stolen the coat earlier in the day, before Stella made her parcel? If that was so, it went some way to weakening the case against her. But it was not so. It was not so because it was utterly improbable that Janie should steal a coat in the afternoon and return to the house the same evening.

"Start at the beginning," Smiley muttered, a little sententiously to the crested paper on his lap. "Janie stole the coat at the same time as she stole the beads—that is, after Stella was dead. Therefore either the coat was not packed with the other clothes, or . . ."

Or what? *Or somebody else, somebody who was not Stella Rode, packed up the clothes after Stella had died and before Dorothy D'Arcy and Mr. Cardew went round to North Fields on Friday morning. And why the devil,* thought Smiley, *should anyone do that?*

It had been one of Smiley's cardinal principles in research, whether among the incunabula of an obscure poet or the laboriously gathered fragments of intelligence, not to proceed beyond the evidence. A fact, once logically arrived at, should not be extended beyond its natural significance. Accordingly he did not speculate with the remarkable discovery he had made, but turned his mind to the most obscure problem of all: motive for murder.

He began writing:

"Dorothy D'Arcy—resentment after refugee fiasco. As a motive for murder—definitely thin." Yet why did she seem to go out of her way to sing Stella's praises?

"Felix D'Arcy—resented Stella Rode for not observing Carne's standards. As a motive for murder—ludicrous.

"Shane Hecht—hatred.

"Terence Fielding—in a sane world, no conceivable motive."

Yet was it a sane world? Year in year out they must share the same life, say the same things to the same people, sing the same hymns. They had no money, no hope. The world changed, fashion changed; the women saw it second-hand in the glossy papers, took in their dresses and pinned up their hair, and hated their husbands a little more. Shane Hecht—did she kill Stella Rode? Did she conceal in the sterile omniscience of her huge body not only hatred and jealousy, but the courage to kill? Was she frightened for her stupid husband, frightened of Rode's promotion, of his cleverness? Was she really so angry when Stella refused to take part in the rat race of gentility?

Rigby was right—it was impossible to know. You had to be ill, you had to be sick to understand, you had to be there in the sanatorium, not for weeks, but for years, had to be one in the line of white beds, to know the smell of their food and the greed in their eyes. You had to hear it and see it, to be part of it, to know their rules and recognise their transgressions. This world was compressed into a mould of anomalous conventions: blind, pharasaical but real.

Yet some things were written plain enough; the curious bond which tied Felix D'Arcy and Terence Fielding despite their mutual dislike; D'Arcy's reluctance to discuss the night of the murder; Fielding's evident preference for Stella Rode rather than her husband; Shane Hecht's contempt for everyone.

He could not get Shane out of his mind. If Carne were a rational place, and somebody had to die, then

Shane Hecht should clearly be the one. She was a depository of other people's secrets, she had an infallible sense for weakness. Had she not found even Smiley out? She had taunted him with his wretched marriage, she had played with him for her own pleasure. Yes, she was an admirable candidate for murder.

But why on earth should Stella die? Why and how? Who tied up the parcel after her death? And why?

He tried to sleep, but could not. Finally, as the Abbey clock chimed three, he put the light on again and sat up. The room was much warmer and at first Smiley wondered if someone had switched on the central heating in the middle of the night, after it had been off all day. Then he became aware of the sound of rain outside; he went to the window and parted the curtains. A steady rain was falling; by tomorrow the snow would be washed away. Two policemen walked slowly down the road; he could hear the squelch of their boots as they trod in the melting snow. Their wet capes glistened in the arc of the street lamp.

And suddenly he seemed to hear Rigby's voice: "Blood everywhere. Whoever killed her must have been covered in it." And then Mad Janie calling to him across the moonlit snow: "Janie seed 'im . . . silver wings like fishes . . . flying on the wind . . . there's not many seen the devil fly. . . ." Of course: the parcel! He remained a long time at the window, watching the rain. Finally, content at last, he climbed back into bed and fell asleep.

He tried to telephone Miss Brimley throughout the morning. Each time she was out and he left no message. Eventually, at about midday, he spoke to her:

"George, I'm terribly sorry—some missionary is in London—I had to go for an interview and I've got a Baptist Conference this afternoon. They've both got to be in this week. Will first thing tomorrow do?"

"Yes," said Smiley. "I'm sure it will." There was no particular hurry. There were one or two ends he wanted to tie up that afternoon, anyway.

XII

Uncomfortable Words

He enjoyed the bus. The conductor was a very surly man with a great deal to say about the bus company, and why it lost money. Gently encouraged by Smiley, he expanded wonderfully so that by the time they arrived at Sturminster he had transformed the Directors of the Dorset and General Traction Company into a herd of Gadarene swine charging into the abyss of voluntary bankruptcy. The conductor directed Smiley to the Sturminster kennels, and when he alighted in the tiny village he set out confidently towards a group of cottages which stood about a quarter of a mile beyond the church, on the Okeford road.

He had a nasty feeling he wasn't going to like Mr. Harriman. The very fact that D'Arcy had described him as a superior type of person inclined Smiley against him. Smiley was not opposed to social distinctions but he liked to make his own.

A notice stood at the gate: *"Sturminster Kennels, proprietor, C. F. Reid-Harriman, Veterinary Surgeon. Breeder of Alsatian and Labrador Dogs. Boarding."*

A narrow path led to what seemed to be a backyard. There was washing everywhere, shirts, underclothes and sheets, most of it khaki. There was a rich smell of dog. There was a rusted hand-pump with a dozen or so dog leads draped over it, and there was a small girl. She watched him sadly as he picked his way through the thick mud towards the door. He pulled on the bell-rope and waited. He tried again, and the child said:

"It doesn't work. It's bust. It's been bust for years."

"Is anyone at home?" Smiley asked.

"I'll see," she replied coolly, and after another long look at him she walked round the side of the house and disappeared from view. Then Smiley heard from inside the house the sound of someone approaching, and a moment later the door opened.

"Good day to you." He had sandy hair and a moustache. He wore a khaki shirt and a khaki tie of a lighter shade; old Service dress trousers and a tweed jacket with leather buttons.

"Mr. Harriman?"

"Major," he replied lightly. "Not that it matters, old boy. What can we do for you?"

"I'm thinking of buying an Alsatian," Smiley replied, "as a guard dog."

"Surely. Come in, won't you. Lady wife's out. Ignore the child: she's from next door. Just hangs around; likes the dogs." He followed Harriman into the living room and they sat down. There was no fire.

"Where are you from?" Harriman asked.

"I'm staying at Carne at the moment; my father lives over at Dorchester. He's getting on and he's nervous, and he wants me to find him a good dog. There's a gardener to look after it in the daytime, feed it and exercise it and so on. The gardener doesn't live in at night, of course, and it's at night that the old man gets so worried. I've been meaning to get him a dog for some time—this recent business at Carne rather brought it home to me." Harriman ignored the hint.

"Gardener good chap?"

"Yes, very."

"You don't want anything brilliant," said Harriman. "You want a good, steady type. I'd take a bitch if I were you." His hands were dark brown, his wrists too. His handkerchief was tucked into his cuff. Smiley noticed that his wrist-watch faced inwards, conforming with the obscure rites of the military *demimonde* from which he seemed to come.

"What will it do, a dog like that? Will it attack, or what?"

"Depends how she's trained, old boy; depends how she's trained. She'll warn, though; that's the main thing. Frighten the fellers away. Shove a notice up, 'Fierce Dog,' let her sniff at the tradesmen a bit and the word will get around. You won't get a burglar within a mile of the place."

They walked out into the garden again, and Harriman led the way to an enclosure with half a dozen Alsatian puppies yapping furiously at them through the wire.

"They're good little beasts, all of them," he shouted. "Game as hell." He unlocked the door and finally emerged with a plump bitch puppy chewing fiercely at his jacket.

"This little lady might do you," he said. "We can't show her—she's too dark."

Smiley pretended to hesitate, allowed Harriman to persuade him and finally agreed. They went back into the house.

"I'd like to pay a deposit," said Smiley, "and collect her in about ten days. Would that be all right?" He gave Harriman a cheque for five pounds and again they sat down, Harriman foraging in his desk for inoculation certificates and pedigrees. Then Smiley said:

"It's a pity Mrs. Rode didn't have a dog, isn't it? I mean, it might have saved her life."

"Oh, she *had* a dog, but she had it put down just before she was killed," said Harriman. "Damned odd story between ourselves. She was devoted to the beast. Odd little mongrel, bit of everything, but she loved it. Brought it here one day with some tale about it biting the postman, got me to put it down—said it was dangerous. It wasn't anything of the sort. Some friends of mine in Carne made enquiries. No complaints anywhere. Postman liked the brute. Damned silly sort of lie to tell in a small community. Bound to be found out."

"Why on earth did she tell it then?"

Harriman made a gesture which particularly irritated Smiley. He ran his forefinger down the length of his nose, then flicked either side of his absurd moustache very quickly. There was something shamefaced about the whole movement, as if he were assuming the ways of senior officers, and fearful of rebuke.

"She was trouble," he said crisply. "I can spot 'em. I've had a few in the regiment, wives who are trouble. Little simpering types. Butter-wouldn't-melt, holier-than-thou. Arrange the flowers in the church and all that—pious as you please. I'd say she was the hysterical kind, self-dramatising, weeping all over the house for days on end. Anything for a bit of drama."

"Was she popular?" Smiley offered him a cigarette.

"Shouldn't think so. Thanks. She wore black on Sundays, I gather. Typical. We used to call them 'crows' out East, the ones who wore black—Sunday virgins. They were O.D. mostly—other denominations. Not C. of E.—some were Romans, mind. . . . I hope I'm not . . ."

"Not at all."

"You never know, do you? Can't stand 'em myself; no prejudice, but I don't like Romans—that's what my old father used to say."

"Did you know her husband?"

"Not so well, poor devil, not so well."

Harriman, Smiley reflected, seemed to have a great deal more sympathy for the living than the dead. Perhaps soldiers were like that. He wouldn't know.

"He's terribly cut up, I hear. Dreadful shock—fortunes of war, eh?" he added and Smiley nodded. "He's the other type. Humble origin, good officer qualities, credit to the mess. Those are the ones that cut up most, the ones women get at."

They walked along the path to the gate. Smiley said goodbye, and promised to return in a week or so to collect the puppy. As he walked away Harriman called to him:

"Oh—incidentally . . ."

Smiley stopped and turned round.

"I'll pay that cheque in, shall I, and credit you with the amount?"

"Of course," said Smiley. "That will do very well," and he made his way to the bus stop pondering on the strange byways of the military mind.

The same bus took him back to Carne, the same conductor railed against his employers, the same driver drove the entire distance in second gear. He got out at the station and made his way to the red-brick Tabernacle. Gently opening the Gothic door, made of thickly-varnished ochre pine, he stepped inside. An elderly woman in an apron was polishing the heavy brass chandelier which hung over the centre aisle. He waited a moment, then tiptoed up to her and asked for the Minister. She pointed towards the vestry door. Obeying her mimed directions, he crossed to it, knocked and waited. A tall man in a clerical collar opened the door.

"I'm from the *Christian Voice*," said Smiley quietly. "Can I have a word with you?"

Mr. Cardew led him through the side entrance and into a small vegetable garden, carefully tilled, with bright yellow paths running between the empty beds. The sun shone through the crisp air. It was a cold, beautiful day. They crossed the garden and entered a paddock. The ground was hard despite last night's rain, and the grass short. They strolled side by side, talking as they went.

"This is Lammas Land, belonging to the School. We hold our fêtes here in the summer. It's very practical."

Cardew seemed a little out of character. Smiley, who had a rather childish distrust of clergymen, had expected a Wesleyan hammer, a wordy, forbidding man with a taste for imagery.

"Miss Brimley, our editor, sent me," Smiley began. "Mrs. Rode subscribed to our journal; her family has taken it since it began. She was almost a part of the family. We wanted to write an obituary about her work for the Church."

"I see."

"I managed to have a word with her husband; we wanted to be sure to strike the right note."

"What did he say?"

"He said I should speak to you about her work— her refugee work particularly."

They walked on in silence for a while, then Cardew said, "She came from up North, near Derby. Her father used to be a man of substance in the North— though money never altered him."

"I know."

"I've known the family for years, off and on. I saw her old father before the funeral."

"What may I say about her work for the Church, her influence on the Chapel community here? May I say she was universally loved?"

"I'm afraid," said Cardew, after a slight pause, "that I don't hold much with that kind of writing, Mr. Smiley. People are never universally loved, even when they're dead." His North Country accent was strong.

"Then what may I say?" Smiley persisted.

"I don't know," Cardew replied evenly. "And when I don't know, I usually keep quiet. But since you're good enough to ask me, I've never met an angel, and Stella Rode was no exception."

"But was she not a leading figure in refugee work?"

"Yes. Yes, she was."

"And did she not encourage others to make similar efforts?"

"Of course. She was a good worker."

They walked on together in silence. The path across the field led downwards, then turned and followed a stream which was almost hidden by the tangled gorse and hawthorn on either side. Beyond the stream was a row of stark elm trees, and behind them the familiar outline of Carne.

"Is that all you wanted to ask me?" said Cardew suddenly.

"No," replied Smiley. "Our editor was very worried by a letter she received from Mrs. Rode just before her death. It was a kind of . . . accusation. We put the matter before the police. Miss Brimley reproaches herself in some way for not having been able to help her. It's illogical, perhaps, but there it is. I would like to be able to assure her that there was no connection between Stella Rode's death and this letter. That is another reason for my visit. . . ."

"Whom did the letter accuse?"

"Her husband."

"I should tell your Miss Brimley," said Cardew slowly, and with some emphasis, "that she has nothing whatever for which to reproach herself."

XIII

The Journey Home

It was Monday evening. At about the time that Smiley returned to his hotel after his interview with Mr. Cardew, Tim Perkins, the Head of Fielding's house, was taking his leave of Mrs. Harlowe, who taught him the 'cello. She was a kindly woman, if neurotic, and it distressed her to see him so worried. He was quite the best pupil that Carne had sent her, and she liked him.

"You played foully today, Tim," she said as she wished him goodbye at the door, "quite foully. You needn't tell me—you've only got one more Half and you still haven't got three passes in A Level and you've got to get your remove, and you're in a tizz. We won't practise next Monday if you don't want—just come and have buns and we'll play some records."

"Yes, Mrs. Harlowe." He strapped his music-case on to the carrier of his bicycle.

"Lights working, Tim?"

"Yes, Mrs. Harlowe."

"Well, don't try and beat the record tonight, Tim. You've plenty of time till Boys' Tea. Remember the lane's still quite slippery from the snow."

Perkins said nothing. He pushed the bicycle on to the gravel path and started towards the gate.

"Haven't you forgotten something, Tim?"

"Sorry, Mrs. Harlowe."

He turned back and shook hands with her in the doorway. She always insisted on that.

"Look, Tim, what *is* the matter? Have you done something silly? You can tell me, can't you? I'm not Staff, you know."

Perkins hesitated, then said:

"It's just exams., Mrs. Harlowe."

"Are your parents all right? No trouble at home?"

"No, Mrs. Harlowe; they're fine." Again he hesitated, then: "Good night, Mrs. Harlowe."

"Good night."

She watched him close the gate behind him and cycle off down the narrow lane. He would be in Carne in quarter of an hour; it was downhill practically all the way.

Usually he loved the ride home. It was the best moment of the week. But tonight he hardly noticed it. He rode fast, as he always did; the hedge raced against the dark sky and the rabbits scuttled from the beam of his lamp, but tonight he hardly noticed them.

He would have to tell somebody. He should have told Mrs. Harlowe; he wished he had. She'd know what to do. Mr. Snow would have been all right, but he wasn't up to him for science any longer, he was up to Rode. That was half the trouble. That and Fielding.

He could tell True—yes, that's who he'd tell, he'd tell True. He'd go to Miss Truebody tonight after evening surgery and he'd tell her the truth. His father would never get over it, of course, because it meant failure and perhaps disgrace. It meant not getting to Sandhurst at the end of next Half, it meant more money they couldn't afford. . . .

He was coming to the steepest part of the hill. The hedge stopped on one side and instead there was a marvellous view of Sawley Castle against the night sky, like a backcloth for *Macbeth*. He loved acting—he wished the Master let them act at Carne.

He leant forward over the handlebars and allowed himself to gather speed to go through the shallow ford at the bottom of the hill. The cold air bit into his face, and for a moment he almost forgot. . . . Suddenly he braked; felt the bike skid wildly beneath him.

Something was wrong; there was a light ahead, a flashing light, and a familiar voice calling to him urgently across the darkness.

XIV

The Quality Of Mercy

The Public Schools Committee for Refugee Relief (Patroness: Sarah, Countess of Sawley) has an office in Belgrave Square. It is not at all clear whether this luxurious situation is designed to entice the wealthy or encourage the dispossessed—or, as some irreverent voices in Society whispered, to provide the Countess of Sawley with an inexpensive *pied-à-terre* in the West End of London. The business of assisting refugees has been suitably relegated to the south of the river, to one of those untended squares in Kennington which are part of London's architectural schizophrenia. York Gardens, as the square is called, will one day be discovered by the world, and its charm lost, but go there now, and you may see real children playing hopscotch in the road, and their mothers, shod in bedroom slippers, abusing them from doorways.

Miss Brimley, despatched on her way by Smiley's telephone call the previous morning, had the rare gift of speaking to children as if they were human beings, and thus discovered without difficulty the dilapidated, unnamed house which served the Committee as a collecting centre. With the assistance of seven small boys, she pulled on the bell and waited patiently. At last she heard the clatter of feet descending an uncarpeted staircase, and the door was opened by a very beautiful girl.

They looked at one another with approval for a moment.

"I'm sorry to be a nuisance," Miss Brimley began, "but a friend of mine in the country has asked me to make some enquiries about a parcel of clothes that was sent up a day or two ago. She's made rather a stupid mistake."

"Oh, goodness, how awful," said the girl pleasantly. "Would you like to come in? Everything's frightfully chaotic, I'm afraid, and there's nothing to sit on, but we can give you powdered coffee in a mug."

Miss Brimley followed her in, closing the door firmly on the seven children, who were edging gently forward in her wake. She was in the hall, and everywhere she looked there were parcels of every kind, some wrapped in jute with smart labels, some in brown paper, torn and clumsy, some in crates and laundry baskets, old suitcases and even an antiquated cabin trunk with a faded yellow label on it which read: "Not wanted on voyage."

The girl led the way upstairs to what was evidently the office, a large room containing a deal table littered with correspondence, and a kitchen chair. An oil stove sputtered in one corner, and an electric kettle was steaming in a melancholy way beside it.

"I'm sorry," said the girl as they entered the room, "but there just isn't anywhere to talk downstairs. I mean, one can't talk on one leg like Incas. Or isn't it Incas? Perhaps it's Afghans. However did you find us?"

"I went to your West End office first," Miss Brimley replied, "and they told me I should come and see you. I think they were rather cross. After that I relied on children. They always know the way. You are Miss Dawney, aren't you?"

"Lord, no. I'm the sort of daily help. Jill Dawney's gone to see the Customs people at Rotherhide—she'll be back at tea time if you want to see her."

"Gracious, my dear, I'm sure I shan't keep you two minutes. A friend of mine who lives in Carne— ("Goodness! How grand," said the girl) she's a sort of cousin really, but it's simpler to call her a friend, isn't it?—gave an old grey dress to the refugee people last Thursday and now she's convinced she left her brooch pinned to the bodice. I'm sure she hasn't done anything of the sort, mind you—she's a scatter-brain creature—but she rang me yesterday morning in a dreadful state and made me promise to come round at once and ask. I couldn't come yesterday, unfortunately—tied to my little paper from dawn till dusk. But I gather you're a bit behind, so it won't be too late?"

"Gosh, no! We're miles behind. That's all the stuff downstairs, waiting to be unpacked and sorted. It comes from the voluntary reps at each school—sometimes boys and sometimes Staff—and they put all the clothes together and send them up in big parcels, either by train or ordinary mail, usually by train. We sort them here before sending abroad."

"That's what I gathered from Jane. As soon as she realised she'd made this mistake she got hold of the woman doing the collecting and sending, but of course it was too late. The parcel had gone."

"How frantic. . . . Do you know when the parcel was sent off?"

"Yes. On Friday morning."

"From Carne? Train or post?"

Miss Brimley had been dreading this question, but she made a guess:

"Post, I believe."

Darting past Miss Brimley, the girl foraged among the pile of papers on her desk and finally produced a stiff-backed exercise book with a label on it marked "Ledger." Opening it at random, she whisked quickly back and forth through the pages, licking the tip of one finger now and then in a harassed sort of way.

"Wouldn't have arrived till yesterday at the earliest," she said. "We certainly won't have opened it yet. Honestly, I don't know how we shall *ever* cope, and with Easter coming up we shall just get worse and worse. On top of that, half our stuff is rotting in the Customs sheds—hullo, here we are!" She pushed the ledger over to Miss Brimley, her slim finger pointing to a pencilled entry in the central column: "Carne, parcel post, 27 lb."

"I wonder," said Miss Brimley, "whether you would mind awfully if we had a quick look inside?"

They went downstairs to the hall.

"It's not quite as hideous as it looks," the girl called over her shoulder. "All the Monday lot will be nearest the door."

"How do you know where they come from if you can't read the postmark?" asked Miss Brimley as the girl began to forage among the parcels.

"We issue the volunteer reps. with our printed labels. The labels have an originator's number on. In other cases we just ask them to write the name of the school in capitals on the outside. You see, we simply can't allow covering letters; it would be *too* desperate. When we get a parcel all we have to do is send off a printed card acknowledging with thanks receipt of a parcel of such and such a date weighing so and so much. People who aren't reps won't send parcels to this address, you see—they'll send to the advertised address in Belgrave Square."

"Does the system work?"

"No," replied the girl, "it doesn't. The reps either forget to use our labels or they run out and can't be bothered to tell us. Ten days later they ring up in a rage because they haven't had an acknowledgement. Reps. change, too, without letting us know, and the packing and labelling instructions don't get passed on. Sometimes the boys will suddenly decide to do it themselves, and no one tells them the way to go about it. Lady Sarah gets as mad as a snake if parcels turn up at Head Office—they all have to be carted over here for repacking and inventories."

"I see." Miss Brimley watched anxiously as the girl foraged among the parcels, still talking.

"Did you say your friend actually *taught* at Carne? She must be terribly grand. I wonder what the Prince is like: he looks rather soft in his photographs. My cousin went to Carne—he's an utter wet. Do you know what he told me? During Ascot week they all . . . Hello!

Here we are!" The girl stood up, a large square parcel in her arms, and carried it to a table which stood in the shadow of the staircase. Miss Brimley, standing beside her as she began carefully to untie the stout twine, looked curiously at the printed label. In its top left-hand corner was stamped the symbol which the Committee had evidently allocated to Carne: C4. After the four the letter B had been written in with ballpoint pen.

"What does the B mean?" asked Miss Brimley.

"Oh, that's a local arrangement at Carne. Miss D'Arcy's the rep there, but they've done so well recently that she co-opted a friend to help with despatch. When we acknowledge we always mention whether it was A or B. B must be terribly keen, whoever she is."

Miss Brimley forebore from enquiring what proportion of the parcels from Carne had originated from Miss D'Arcy, and what proportion from her anonymous assistant.

The girl removed the string and turned the parcel upside down in order to liberate the overlap of wrapping paper. As she did so Miss Brimley caught sight of a faint brown smudge, no more, about the size of a shilling, near the join. It was consistent with her essential rationalism that she should search for any explanation other than that which so loudly presented itself. The girl continued the work of unwrapping, saying suddenly: "I say, Carne was where they had that dreadful murder, wasn't it—that master's wife who got killed by the gypsy? It really *is* awful, isn't it, how much of that kind of thing goes on? Hm! Thought as much," she remarked, suddenly interrupting herself. She had removed the outer paper, and was about to unwrap the bundle inside when her attention was evidently arrested by the appearance of the inner parcel.

"What?" Miss Brimley said quickly.

The girl laughed. "Oh, only the packing," she said. "The C4Bs are usually so neat—quite the best we get. This is quite different. Not the same person at all. Must be a stand-in. I thought so from the outside."

"How can you be so sure?"

"Oh, it's like handwriting. We can tell." She

laughed again, and without more ado removed the last wrapping. "Grey dress, you said, didn't you? Let's see." With both hands she began picking clothes from the top of the pile and laying them to either side. She was nearly half way through when she exclaimed "Well, *honestly!* They must be having a brain-storm," and drew from the bundle of partworn clothes a transparent plastic mackintosh, a very old pair of leather gloves, and a pair of rubber overshoes.

Miss Brimley was holding the edge of the table very tightly. The palms of her hands were throbbing.

"Here's a cape. Damp, too," the girl added in disgust, and tossed the offending articles on to the floor beside the table. Miss Brimley could only think of Smiley's letter: "Whoever killed her must have been covered in blood." Yes, and whoever killed her wore a plastic cape and a hood, rubber overshoes and those old leather gloves with the terra-cotta stains. Whoever killed Stella Rode had not chanced upon her in the night, but had plotted long ahead, had waited. "Yes," thought Miss Brimley, "had waited for the long nights."

The girl was talking to her again: "I'm afraid it really isn't here."

"No, my dear," Miss Brimley replied, "I see that. Thank you. You've been very sweet." Her voice faltered for a moment, then she managed to say: "I think, my dear, you should leave the parcel exactly as it is now, the wrapping and everything in it. Something very dreadful has happened, and the police will want to . . . know about it and see the parcel. . . . You must trust me, my dear—things aren't quite what they seem. . . ." And somehow she escaped to the comforting freedom of York Gardens and the large-eyed wonder of its waiting children.

She went to a telephone box. She got through to the Sawley Arms and asked a very bored receptionist for Mr. Smiley. Total silence descended on the line until the Trunks operator asked her to put in another three and sixpence. Miss Brimley replied sharply that all she had so far had for her money was a three-minute vacuum; this was followed by the unmistakable sound of the operator sucking her teeth, and then, quite suddenly, by George Smiley's voice:

"George, it's Brim. A plastic mackintosh, a cape, rubber overshoes and some leather gloves that look as though they're stained with blood. Smudges on some of the wrapping paper too by the look of it."

A pause.

"Handwriting on the outside of the parcel?"

"None. The Charity organisers issue printed labels."

"Where is the stuff now? Have you got it?"

"No. I've told the girl to leave everything exactly as it is. It'll be all right for an hour or two. . . . George, are you there?"

"Yes."

"Who did it? Was it the husband?"

"I don't know. I just don't know."

"Do you want me to do anything—about the clothes, I mean? Phone Sparrow or anything?"

"No. I'll see Rigby at once. Goodbye, Brim. Thanks for ringing."

She put back the receiver. He sounded strange, she thought. He seemed to lose touch sometimes. As if he'd switched off.

She walked northwest towards the Embankment. It was long after ten o'clock—the first time she'd been late for Heaven knows how long. She had better take a taxi. Being a frugal woman, however, she took a bus.

Ailsa Brimley did not believe in emergencies, for she enjoyed a discipline of mind uncommon in men and even rarer in women. The greater the emergency, the greater her calm. John Landsbury had remarked upon it: "You have sales resistance to the dramatic, Brim; the rare gift of contempt for what is urgent. I know of a dozen people who would pay you five thousand a year for telling them everyday that what is important is seldom urgent. Urgent equals ephemeral, and ephemeral equals unimportant."

She got out of the bus, carefully putting the ticket in the rubbish compartment. As she stood in the warm sunlight of the street she caught sight of the hoardings advertising the first edition of the evening papers. If it hadn't been for the sun, she might never have looked; but the sun dazzled her and made her glance downwards. And so she did see; she read it in the plump black of the wet newsprint, in the prepacked hysteria of Fleet Street: "All-night search for missing Carne boy."

XV

The Road To Fielding

Smiley put down the receiver and walked quickly past the reception desk towards the front door. He must see Rigby at once. Just as he was leaving the hotel he heard his name called. Turning, he saw his old enemy, the night porter, braving the light of day, beckoning to him like Charon with his grey hand.

"They've been on to you from the police station," he observed with undisguised pleasure; "Mr. Rigby wants you, the Inspector. You're to go there at once. At once, see?"

"I'm on my way there now," Smiley replied irritably, and as he pushed his way through the swing doors he heard the old man repeat; "At once, mind; they're waiting for you."

Making his way through the Carne streets, he reflected for the hundredth time on the obscurity of motive in human action: there is no true thing on earth. There is no constant, no dependable point, not even in the purest logic or the most obscure mysticism; least of all in the motives of men when they are moved to act violently.

Had the murderer, now so near discovery, found contentment in the meticulous administration of his plans? For now it was clear beyond a doubt; this was a

113

murder devised to the last detail, even to the weapon inexplicably far from the place of its use; a murder with clues cast to mislead, a murder planned to look un-planned, a murder for a string of beads. Now the mys-tery of the footprints was solved: having put the over-shoes into the parcel, the murderer had walked down the path to the gate, and his own prints had been ob-scured by the subsequent traffic of feet.

Rigby looked tired.

"You've heard the news, sir, I suppose?"

"What news?"

"About the boy, the boy in Fielding's house, miss-ing all night?"

"No." Smiley felt suddenly sick. "No, I've heard nothing."

"Good Lord, I thought you knew! Half-past eight last night Fielding rang us here. Perkins, his head boy, hadn't come back from a music lesson with Mrs. Har-lowe, who lives over to Longemede. We put out an alert and started looking for him. They sent a patrol car along the road he should have come back on—he was cycling, you see. The first time they didn't see anything, but on the way back the driver stopped the car at the bottom of Longemede Hill, just where the water-splash is. It occurred to him the lad might have taken a long run at the water-splash from the top of the hill, and come to grief in the dip. They found him half in the ditch, his bike beside him. Dead."

"Oh, my dear God."

"We didn't let on to the press at first. The boy's parents are in Singapore. The father's an Army officer. Fielding sent them a telegram. We've got on to the War Office, too."

They were silent for a moment, then Smiley asked "How did it happen?"

"We've closed the road and we've been trying to reconstruct the accident. I've got a detective over there now, just having a look. Trouble is, we couldn't do much till the morning. Besides, the men trampled every-where; you can't blame them. It looks as though he must have fallen near the bottom of the hill and hit his head on a stone: his right temple."

"How did Fielding take it?"

"He was very shaken. Very shaken indeed. I wouldn't have believed it, to be quite honest. He just seemed to . . . give up. There was a lot that had to be done—telegraph the parents, get in touch with the boy's uncle at Windsor, and so on. But he just left all that to Miss Truebody, his housekeeper. If it hadn't been for her, I don't know how he'd have managed. I was with him for about half an hour, then he just broke down, completely, and asked to be left alone."

"How do you mean, broke down?" Smiley asked quickly.

"He cried. Wept like a child," said Rigby evenly. "I'd never have thought it."

Smiley offered Rigby a cigarette and took one himself.

"I suppose," he ventured, "it was an accident?"

"I suppose so," Rigby replied woodenly.

"Perhaps," said Smiley, "before we go any further, I'd better give you my news. I was on my way to see you when you rang. I've just heard from Miss Brimley." And in his precise, rather formal way he related all that Ailsa Brimley had told him, and how he had become curious about the contents of the parcel.

Smiley waited while Rigby telephoned to London. Almost mechanically, Rigby described what he wanted done: the parcel and its contents were to be collected and arrangements made to subject them immediately to forensic examination; the surfaces should be tested for fingerprints. He would be coming up to London himself with some samples of a boy's handwriting and an examination paper; he would want the opinion of a handwriting expert. No, he would be coming by train on the 4.25 from Carne, arriving at Waterloo at 8.05. Could a car be sent to the station to collect him? There was silence, then Rigby said testily, "All right, I'll take a ruddy taxi," and rang off rather abruptly. He looked at Smiley angrily for a moment, then grinned, plucked at his ear and said:

"Sorry, sir; getting a bit edgy." He indicated the far wall with his head and added, "Fighting on too many fronts, I suppose. I shall have to tell the Chief about that parcel, but he's out shooting at the moment—only pigeon, with a couple of friends, he won't be long—but I haven't mentioned your presence here in Carne, as a matter of fact, and if you don't mind I'll . . ."

"Of course," Smiley cut in quickly. "It's much simpler if you keep me out of it."

"I shall tell him it was just a routine enquiry. We shall have to mention Miss Brimley later . . . but there's no point in making things worse, is there?"

"No."

"I shall have to let Janie go, I suppose. . . . She was right, wasn't she? Silver wings in the moonlight."

"I wouldn't—no, I wouldn't let her go, Rigby," said Smiley with unaccustomed vehemence. "Keep her with you as long as you can possibly manage. No more accidents, for Heaven's sake. We've had enough."

"Then you don't believe Perkins' death was an accident?"

"Good Lord, no," cried Smiley suddenly, "and nor do you, do you?"

"I've put a detective on to it," Rigby replied coolly. "I can't take the case myself. I shall be needed on the Rode murder. The Chief will have to call the Yard in now; there'll be hell to pay I can tell you. He thought it was all over bar the shouting."

"And in the meantime?"

"In the meantime, sir, I'm going to do my damnedest to find out who killed Stella Rode."

"If," said Smiley slowly, "if you find fingerprints on that mackintosh, which I doubt, will you have anything . . . local . . . to compare them with?"

"We've got Rode's, of course, and Janie's."

"But not Fielding's?"

Rigby hesitated.

"As a matter of fact, we have," he said at last.

"From long ago. But nothing to do with this kind of thing."

"It was during the war," said Smiley. "His brother told me. Up in the North. It was hushed up, wasn't it?"

Rigby nodded. "So far as I heard, only the D'Arcys knew; and the Master, of course. It happened in the holidays—some Air Force boy. The Chief was very helpful. . . ."

Smiley shook hands with Rigby and made his way down the familiar pine staircase. He noticed again the vaguely institutional smell of floor polish and carbolic soap, like the smell at Fielding's house.

He walked slowly back towards the Sawley Arms. At the point where he should have turned left to his hotel, however, he hesitated, then seemed to change his mind. Slowly, almost reluctantly, he crossed the road to the Abbey Close, and walked along the southern edge towards Fielding's house. He looked worried, almost frightened.

XVI

A Taste For Music

Miss Truebody opened the door. The rims of her eyes were pink, as though she had been weeping.

"I wonder if I might see Mr. Fielding? To say goodbye."

She hesitated: "Mr. Fielding's very upset. I doubt whether he'll want to see anyone." He followed her into the hall and watched her go to the study door. She knocked, inclined her head, then gently turned the handle and let herself in. It was a long time before she returned. "He'll be out shortly," she said, without looking at him. "Will you take off your coat?" She waited while he struggled out of his overcoat, then took it from him and hung it beside the Van Gogh chair. They stood together in silence, both looking towards the study door.

Then, quite suddenly, Fielding was standing in the half-open doorway, unshaven and in his shirt-sleeves. "For Christ's sake," he said thickly. "What do you want?"

"I just wanted to say goodbye, Fielding, and to offer you my condolences."

Fielding looked at him hard for a moment; he was leaning heavily against the doorway; "Well, goodbye. Thank you for calling." He waved one hand vaguely in the air. "You needn't have bothered really, need you?"

he added rudely. "You could have sent me a card, couldn't you?"

"I could have done, yes; it just seemed so very tragic, when he was so near success."

"What do you mean? What the devil do you mean?"

"I mean in his work . . . the improvement. Simon Snow was telling me all about it. Amazing really, the way Rode brought him on."

A long silence, then Fielding spoke: "Goodbye, Smiley. Thanks for coming." He was turning back into the study as Smiley called:

"Not at all . . . not at all. I suppose poor Rode must have been bucked with those exam. results, too. I mean it was more or less a matter of life and death for Perkins, passing that exam., wasn't it? He wouldn't have got his remove next Half if he'd failed in science. They might have superannuated him, I suppose, even though he was head of the house; then he couldn't have sat for the Army. Poor Perkins, he had a lot to thank Rode for, didn't he? And you, too, Fielding, I'm sure. You must have helped him wonderfully . . . both of you did, you and Rode; Rode and Fielding. His parents ought to know that. They're rather hard up, I gather; the father's in the Army, isn't he, in Singapore? It must have been a great effort keeping the boy at Carne. It will comfort them to know how much was done for him, won't it, Fielding?"

Smiley was very pale. "You've heard the latest, I suppose," he continued. "About that wretched gypsy woman who killed Stella Rode? They've decided she's fit to plead. I suppose they'll hang her. That'll be the third death, won't it? You know, I'll tell you an odd thing—just between ourselves, Fielding. I don't believe she did it. Do you? I don't believe she did it at all."

He was not looking at Fielding. He had clasped his little hands tightly behind his back, and he stood with his shoulders bowed and his head inclined to one side, as though listening for an answer.

Fielding seemed to feel Smiley's words like a physical pain. Slowly he shook his head:

"No," he said. "No. Carne killed them; it was Carne. It could only happen here. It's the game we play: the exclusion game. Divide and rule!" He looked Smiley full in the face, and shouted: "Now for God's sake go! You've got what you want, haven't you? You can pin me on your little board, can't you?" And then, to Smiley's distress, he began sobbing in great uncontrollable gulps, holding his hand across his brow. He appeared suddenly grotesque, stemming the childish tears with his chalky hand, his cumbersome feet turned inwards. Gently, Smiley coaxed him back into the study, gently sat him before the dead fire. Then he began talking to him softly and with compassion.

"If what I think is true, there isn't much time," he began. "I want you to tell me about Tim Perkins— about the exam."

Fielding, his face buried in his hands, nodded.

"He would have failed, wouldn't he? He would have failed and not got his Remove; he'd have had to leave." Fielding was silent. "After the exam. that day, Rode gave him the writing case to bring here, the case that contained the papers; Rode was doing chapel duty that week and wouldn't be going home before dinner, but he wanted to correct the papers that night, after his dinner with you."

Fielding took his hands from his face and leant back in his chair, his great head tilted back, his eyes closed. Smiley continued:

"Perkins came home, and that evening he brought the case to you, as Rode told him to, for safe keeping. Perkins, after all, was head of your house, a responsible boy. . . . He gave you the case and you asked him how he'd done in the exam."

"He wept," said Fielding suddenly. "He wept as only a child can."

"And after breaking down he told you he had cheated? That he had looked up the answers and copied them on to his paper. Is that right? And after the murder of Stella Rode he remembered what else he had seen in the suitcase?"

Fielding was standing up. "No! Don't you see?

Tim wouldn't have cheated to save his life! That's the whole point, the whole bloody irony of it," he shouted. "He never cheated at all. *I* cheated for him."

"But you couldn't! You couldn't copy his handwriting!"

"He wrote with a ball-pen. It was only formulae and diagrams. When he'd gone, and left me alone with the case, I looked at his paper. It was hopeless—he'd only done two out of seven questions. So I cheated for him. I just cribbed them from the science book, and wrote them with blue ballpoint, the kind we all use. Abbots' sell them. I copied his hand as best I could. It only needed about three lines of figures. The rest was diagrams."

"Then it was you who opened the case? You who saw . . ."

"Yes. It was me, I tell you, not Tim! He couldn't cheat to save his life! But Tim paid for it, don't you see? When the marks were published Tim must have known something was wrong with them. After all, he'd only attempted two questions out of seven and yet he'd got sixty-one per cent. But he knew *nothing* else, *nothing!*"

For a long time neither spoke. Fielding was standing over Smiley, exultant with the relief of sharing his secret, and Smiley was looking vaguely past him, his face drawn in deep concentration.

"And of course," he said finally, "when Stella was murdered, you knew who had done it."

"Yes," replied Fielding. "I knew that Rode had killed her."

Fielding poured himself a brandy and gave one to Smiley. He seemed to have recovered his self-control. He sat down and looked at Smiley thoughtfully for a time.

"I've got no money," he said at last. "None. Nobody knows that except the Master. Oh, they know I'm more or less broke, but they don't know *how* broke. Long ago I made an ass of myself. I got into trouble. It was in the war, when staff was impossible. I had a boys'

house and was practically running the school—D'Arcy
and I. We were running it together, and the Master running us. Then I made an ass of myself. It was during the
holidays. I was up North at the time, giving a course of
talks at an R.A.F. educational place. And I stepped out
of line. Badly. They pulled me in. And along came
D'Arcy wearing his country overcoat and bringing the
Master's terms: Come back to Carne, my dear fellow,
and we'll say no more about it; go on running your
house, my dear fellow, and giving of your wisdom.
There's been no publicity. We know it will never happen again, my dear fellow, and we're dreadfully hard up
for staff. Come back as a temporary. So I did, and I've
been one ever since, going cap in hand to darling
D'Arcy every December asking for my contract to be
renewed. And, of course—no pension. I shall have to
teach at a crammer's. There's a place in Somerset where
they'll take me. I'm seeing their Headmaster in London
on Thursday. It's a sort of breaker's yard for old dons.
The Master had to know, because he gave me a reference."

"That was why you couldn't tell anyone? Because
of Perkins?"

"In a way, yes. I mean they'd want to know all
sorts of things. I did it for Tim, you see. The Governors
wouldn't have liked that much . . . inordinate affection. . . . It looks bad, doesn't it? But it wasn't that
kind of affection, Smiley, not any more. You never
heard him play the 'cello. He wasn't marvellous, but
just sometimes he would play so beautifully, with a kind
of studious simplicity, that was indescribably good. He
was an awkward boy, and when he played well it was
such a surprise. You should have heard him play."

"You didn't want to drag him into it. If you told
the police what you had seen it would ruin Tim too?"

Fielding nodded. "In the whole of Carne, he was
the one thing I loved."

"Loved?" asked Smiley.

"For God's sake," said Fielding in an exhausted
voice, "why not?"

"His parents wanted him to go to Sandhurst; I didn't, I'm afraid. I thought that if I could keep him here another Half or two I might be able to get him a music scholarship. That's why I made him Head of House: I wanted his parents to keep him on because he was doing so well." Fielding paused; "He was a rotten Head of House," he added.

"And what exactly was in the writing-case," Smiley asked, "when you opened it that evening to look at Tim's exam. paper?"

"A sheet of transparent plastic . . . it may have been one of those pack-away cape things—an old pair of gloves, and a pair of home-made galoshes."

"Home-made?"

"Yes. Hacked from a pair of wellington boots, I should think."

"That's all?"

"No. There was a length of heavy cable, I presumed for demonstrating something in his science lessons. It seemed natural enough in winter to carry waterproofs about. Then, after the murder, I realised how he had done it."

"Did you know," asked Smiley, "*why* he had done it?"

Fielding seemed to hesitate: "Rode's a guinea-pig," he began, "the first man we've had from a grammar school. Most of us are old Carnians ourselves, in fact. Focused when we start. Rode wasn't, and Carne thrilled him. The very name Carne means quality, and Rode loved quality. His wife wasn't like that. She had her standards and they were different, but just as good. I used to watch Rode in the Abbey sometimes on Sunday mornings. Tutors sit at the end of pews, right by the aisle, you know. I used to watch his face as the choir processed past him in white and scarlet, and the Master in his doctor's robes and the Governors and Guardians behind him. Rode was drunk—drunk with the pride of Carne. We're heady wine for the grammar school men, you know. It must have hurt him terribly that Stella wouldn't share any of that. You could see it did. The night they came to dinner with me, the night she died,

they argued. I never told anyone, but they did. The
Master had preached a sermon at Compline that evening: 'Hold fast to that which is good.' Rode talked
about it at dinner; he couldn't take much drink, you
know, he wasn't used to it. He was full of this sermon
and of the eloquence of the Master. She never came to
the Abbey—she went to that drab tabernacle by the station. He went on and on about the beauty of the Abbey
service, the dignity, the reverence. She kept quiet till
he'd finished, then laughed, and said: 'Poor old Stan.
You'll always be Stan to me.' I've never seen anyone so
angry as he was then. He went quite pale."

Fielding swept his white hair from his eyes and
went on, with something like the old panache: "I've
watched her, too, at meals. Not just here, but at dinner
parties elsewhere, when we've both been invited. I've
watched her do the simplest things—like eating an apple. She'd peel it in one piece, round and round till the
whole peel fell off. Then she'd cut the apple and dice
the quarters, getting it all ready before she ate it. She
might have been a miner's wife preparing it for her husband. She must have *seen* how people do things here,
but it never occurred to her that she ought to copy
them. I admire that. So do you, I expect. But Carne
doesn't—and Rode didn't; above all, Rode didn't. He'd
watch her, and I think he grew to hate her for not conforming. He came to see her as the bar to his success,
the one factor which would deprive him of a great career. Once he'd reached that conclusion, what could he
do? He couldn't divorce her—that would do him more
harm than remaining married to her. Rode knew what
Carne would think of divorce; we're a Church foundation, remember. So he killed her. He plotted a squalid
murder, and with his little scientist's mind he gave them
all the clues they wanted. Fabricated clues. Clues that
would point to a murderer who didn't exist. But something went wrong; Tim Perkins got sixty-one per cent.
He'd got an impossible mark—he must have cheated.
He'd had the opportunity—he'd had the papers in the
case. Rode put his little mind to it and decided what
had happened: Tim had opened the case and he'd seen

the cape and the boots and the gloves. And the cable. So Rode killed him too."

With surprising energy, Fielding got up and gave himself more brandy. His face was flushed, almost exultant.

Smiley stood up. "When did you say you'll be coming to London? Thursday, wasn't it?"

"Yes. I had arranged to lunch with my crammer man at one of those dreadful clubs in Pall Mall. I always go into the wrong one, don't you? But I'm afraid there's not much point in my seeing him now, is there, if all this is going to come out? Not even a crammer's will take me then."

Smiley hesitated.

"Come and dine with me that evening. Spend the night if you want. I'll ask one or two other people. We'll have a party. You'll feel better by then. We can talk a bit. I might be able to help you . . . for Adrian's sake."

"Thank you. I should like to. Interview apart, I've got some odds and ends to clear up in London, anyway."

"Good. Quarter to eight. Bywater Street, Chelsea, number 9A." Fielding wrote it down in his diary. His hand was quite steady.

"Black tie?" asked Fielding, his pen poised, and some imp made Smiley reply:

"I usually do, but it doesn't matter." There was a moment's silence.

"I suppose," Fielding began tentatively, "that all this *will* come out in the trial, about Tim and me? I'll be ruined if it does, you know, ruined."

"I don't see how they can prevent it."

"I feel much better now, anyway," said Fielding; "much."

With a cursory goodbye, Smiley left him alone. He walked quickly back to the police station, reasonably confident that Terence Fielding was the most accomplished liar he had met for a long time.

XVII

Rabbit Run

He knocked on Rigby's door and walked straight in.

"I'm awfully afraid you'll have to arrest Stanley Rode," he began, and recounted his interview with Fielding.

"I shall have to tell the Chief," said Rigby doubtfully. "Would you like to repeat all that in front of him? If we're going to pull in a Carne master, I think the Chief had better know first. He's just come back. Hang on a minute." He picked up the telephone on his desk and asked for the Chief Constable. A few minutes later they were walking in silence down a carpeted corridor. On either wall hung photographs of rugby and cricket teams, some yellow and faded from the Indian sun, others done in a sepia tint much favoured by Carne photographers in the early part of the century. At intervals along the corridor stood empty buckets of brilliant red, with FIRE printed carefully in white on the outside. At the far end of the corridor was a dark oak door. Rigby knocked and waited. There was silence. He knocked again and was answered with a cry of "Come!"

Two very large spaniels watched them come in. Behind the spaniels, at an enormous desk, Brigadier Havelock, O.B.E., Chief Constable of Carne, sat like a water rat on a raft.

The few strands of white hair which ran laterally

across his otherwise bald head were painstakingly adjusted to cover the maximum area. This gave him an
oddly wet look, as if he had just emerged from the river.
His moustache, which lavishly compensated for the
scarcity of other hair, was yellow and appeared quite
solid. He was a very small man, and he wore a brown
suit and a stiff white collar with rounded corners.

"Sir," Rigby began, "may I introduce Mr. Smiley
from London?"

He came out from behind his desk as if he were
giving himself up, unconvinced but resigned. Then he
pushed out a little, knobbly hand and said, "From London, eh? How d'you do, sir," all at once, as if he'd
learnt it by heart.

"Mr. Smiley's here on a private visit, sir," Rigby
continued. "He is an acquaintance of Mr. Fielding."

"Quite a card, Fielding, quite a card," the Chief
Constable snapped.

"Yes, indeed, sir," said Rigby, and went on:

"Mr. Smiley called on Mr. Fielding just now, sir,
to take his leave before returning to London." Havelock
shot a beady glance at Smiley, as if wondering whether
he were fit to make the journey.

"Mr. Fielding made a kind of statement, which he
substantiated with new evidence of his own. About the
murder, sir."

"Well, Rigby?" he said challengingly. Smiley inter-
vened:

"He said that the husband had done it; Stanley
Rode. Fielding said that when his head boy brought him
Rode's writing-case containing the examination pa-
pers . . ."

"What examination papers?"

"Rode was invigilating that afternoon, you remember. He was also doing chapel duty before going on to
dinner at Fielding's house. As an expediency, he gave
the papers to Perkins to take . . ."

"The boy who had the accident?" Havelock asked.

"Yes."

"You know a lot about it," said Havelock darkly.

"Fielding said that when Perkins brought him the

case, Fielding opened it. He wanted to see how Perkins had done in the science paper. It was vital to the boy's future that he should get his Remove," Smiley went on.

"Oh, work's the only thing now," said Havelock bitterly. "Wasn't the way when I was a boy here, I assure you."

"When Fielding opened the case, the papers were inside. So was a plastic cape, an old pair of leather gloves and a pair of rubber overshoes, cut from wellingtons."

A pause.

"Good God! Good God! Hear that, Rigby? That's what they found in the parcel in London. Good God!"

"Finally, there was a length of cable, heavy cable, in the case as well. It was this writing-case that Rode went back for, you remember, on the night of the murder," Smiley concluded. It was like feeding a child—you couldn't overload the spoon.

There was a very long silence indeed. Then Rigby, who seemed to know his man, said:

"Motive was self-advancement in the profession, sir. Mrs. Rode showed no desire to improve her station, dressed in a slovenly manner and took no part in the religious life of the school."

"Just a minute," said Havelock. "Rode planned the murder from the start, correct?"

"Yes, sir."

"He wanted to make it look like robbery with violence."

"Yes, sir."

"Having collected the writing-case, he walked back to North Fields. Then what does he do?"

"He puts on the plastic cape and hood, overshoes and gloves. He arms himself with the weapon, sir. He lets himself in by the garden gate, crosses the back garden, goes to the front door and rings the bell, sir. His wife comes to the door. He knocks her down, drags her to the conservatory and murders her. He rinses the clothes under the tap and puts them in the parcel. Having sealed the parcel, he walks down the drive this time

to the front gate, following the path, sir, knowing that
his own footprints will soon be obscured by other people's. Having got to the road, where the snow was hard
and showed no prints, he turned round and re-entered
the house, playing the part of the distressed husband,
taking care, when he discovers the body, sir, to put his
own fingerprints over the glove-marks. There was one
article that was too dangerous to send, sir. The
weapon."

"All right, Rigby. Pull him in. Mr. Borrow will
give you a warrant if you want one; otherwise I'll ring
Lord Sawley."

"Yes, sir. And I'll send Sergeant Low to take a full
statement from Mr. Fielding, sir?"

"Why the devil didn't he speak up earlier, Rigby?"

"Have to ask him that, sir," said Rigby woodenly,
and left the room.

"You a Carnian?" Havelock asked, pushing a silver
cigarette-box across the desk.

"No. No, I'm afraid not," Smiley replied.

"How d'you know Fielding?"

"We met at Oxford after the war."

"Queer card, Fielding, very queer. Say your name
was Smiley?"

"Yes."

"There was a fellow called Smiley married Ann
Sercombe, Lord Sawley's cousin. Damned pretty girl,
Ann was, and went and married this fellow. Some funny
little beggar in the Civil Service with an O.B.E. and a
gold watch. Sawley was damned annoyed." Smiley said
nothing. "Sawley's got a son at Carne. Know that?"

"I read it in the press, I think."

"Tell me—this fellow Rode. He's a grammar
school chap, isn't he?"

"I believe so, yes."

"Damned odd business. Experiments never pay,
do they. You can't experiment with tradition."

"No. No, indeed."

"That's the trouble today. Like Africa. Nobody

seems to understand you can't build society overnight. It takes centuries to make a gentleman." Havelock frowned to himself and fiddled with the paper-knife on his desk.

"Wonder how he got his cable into that ditch, the thing he killed her with. He wasn't out of our sight for forty-eight hours after the murder."

"That," said Smiley, "is what puzzles me. So does Jane Lyn."

"What d'you mean?"

"I don't believe Rode would have had the nerve to walk back to the house after killing his wife knowing that Jane Lyn had seen him do it. Assuming, of course, that he *did* know, which seems likely. It's too cool . . . too cool altogether."

"Odd, damned odd," muttered Havelock. He looked at his watch, pushing his left elbow outwards to do so, in a swift equestrian movement which Smiley found comic, and a little sad. The minutes ticked by. Smiley wondered if he should leave, but he had a vague feeling that Havelock wanted his company.

"There'll be a hell of a fuss," said Havelock. "It isn't every day you arrest a Carne tutor for murder." He put down the paper-knife sharply on the desk.

"These bloody journalists ought to be horse-whipped!" he declared. "Look at the stuff they print about the Royal Family. Wicked, wicked!" He got up, crossed the room and sat himself in a leather armchair by the fire. One of the spaniels went and sat at his feet.

"What made him do it, I wonder. What the devil made him do it? His own wife, I mean; a fellow like that." Havelock said this simply, appealing for enlightenment.

"I don't believe," said Smiley slowly, "that we can ever entirely know what makes anyone do anything."

"My God, you're dead right. . . . What do you do for a living, Smiley?"

"After the war I was at Oxford for a bit. Teaching and research. I'm in London now."

"One of those clever coves, eh?"

Smiley wondered when Rigby would return.

"Know anything about this fellow's family? Has he got people, or anything?"

"I think they're both dead," Smiley answered, and the telephone on Havelock's desk rang sharply. It was Rigby. Stanley Rode had disappeared.

XVIII

After The Ball

He caught the 1.30 train to London. He just made it
after an argument at his hotel about the bill. He left a
note for Rigby giving his address and telephone number
in London and asking him to telephone that night when
the laboratory tests were completed. There was nothing
else for him to do in Carne.

As the train pulled slowly out of Carne and one by
one the familiar landmarks disappeared into the cold
February mist, George Smiley was filled with a feeling
of relief. He hadn't wanted to come, he knew that. He'd
been afraid of the place where his wife had spent her
childhood, afraid to see the fields where she had lived.
But he had found nothing, not the faintest memory, neither in the lifeless outlines of Sawley Castle, nor in the
surrounding countryside, to remind him of her. Only
the gossip remained, as it would while the Hechts and
the Havelocks survived to parade their acquaintance
with the first family in Carne.

He took a taxi to Chelsea, carried his suitcase upstairs and unpacked with the care of a man accustomed
to living alone. He thought of having a bath, but decided to ring Ailsa Brimley first. The telephone was by
his bed. He sat on the edge of the bed and dialled the
number. A tinny model-voice sang: "Unipress, good
afternoon," and he asked for Miss Brimley. There was a

long silence, then, "Ah'm afraid Miss Brimley is in conference. Can someone else answer your query?"

Query, thought Smiley. Good God! Why on earth query—why not question or enquiry?

"No," he replied. "Just tell her Mr. Smiley rang." He put back the receiver and went into the bathroom and turned on the hot tap. He was fiddling with his cuff-links when the telephone rang. It was Ailsa Brimley:

"George? I think you'd better come round at once. We've got a visitor. Mr. Rode from Carne. He wants to talk to us." Pulling on his jacket, he ran out into the street and hailed a taxi.

XIX

Disposal Of A Legend

The descending escalator was packed with the staff of Unipress, homebound and heavy-eyed. To them, the sight of a fat, middle-aged gentleman bounding up the adjoining staircase provided unexpected entertainment, so that Smiley was hastened on his way by the jeers of officeboys and the laughter of typists. On the first floor he paused to study an enormous board carrying the titles of a quarter of the national dailies. Finally, under the heading of "Technical and Miscellaneous," he spotted the *Christian Voice*, Room 619. The lift seemed to go up very slowly. Formless music issued from behind its plush, while a boy in a monkey jacket flicked his hips on the heavier beats. The golden doors parted with a sigh, the boy said "Six," and Smiley stepped quickly into the corridor. A moment or two later he was knocking on the door of Room 619. It was opened by Ailsa Brimley.

"George, how nice," she said brightly. "Mr. Rode will be dreadfully pleased to see you." And without any further introduction she led him into her office. In an armchair near the window sat Stanley Rode, tutor of Carne, in a neat black overcoat. As Smiley entered he stood up and held out his hand. "Good of you to come,

134

sir," he said woodenly. "Very." The same flat manner, the same cautious voice.

"How can I help you?" asked Smiley.

They all sat down. Smiley offered Miss Brimley a cigarette and lit it for her.

"It's about this article you're writing about Stella," he began. "I feel awful about it really, because you've been so good to her, and her memory, if you see what I mean. I know you wish well, but I don't want you to write it."

Smiley said nothing, and Ailsa was wise enough to keep quiet. From now on it was Smiley's interview. The silence didn't worry him, but it seemed to worry Rode.

"It wouldn't be right; it wouldn't do at all. Mr. Glaston agreed; I spoke to him yesterday before he left and he agreed. I just couldn't let you write that stuff."

"Why not?"

"Too many people know, you see. Poor Mr. Cardew, I asked him. He knows a lot; and a lot about Stella, so I asked him. He understands why I gave up Chapel too; I couldn't bear to see her going there every Sunday and going down on her knees." He shook his head. "It was all wrong. It just made a fool of your faith."

"What did Mr. Cardew say?"

"He said we should not be the judges. We should let God judge. But I said to him it wouldn't be right, those people knowing her and knowing what she'd done, and then reading all that stuff in the *Voice*. They'd think it was crazy. He didn't seem to see that, he just said to leave it to God. But I can't, Mr. Smiley."

Again no one spoke for a time. Rode sat quite still, save for a very slight rocking movement of his head. Then he began to talk again:

"I didn't believe old Mr. Glaston at first. He said she was bad, but I didn't believe it. They lived up on the hill then, Gorse Hill, only a step from the Tabernacle; Stella and her father. They never seemed to keep servants for long, so she did most of the work. I used to call in Sunday mornings sometimes after church. Stella looked after her father, cooked for him and everything, and I always wondered how I'd ever have the nerve to ask Mr. Glaston for her. The Glastons were big people in Branxome. I was teaching at Grammar School in those days. They let me teach part-time while I read for my degree, and I made up my mind that if I passed the exam, I'd ask her to marry me.

"The Sunday after the results came out I went round to the house after morning service. Mr. Glaston opened the door himself. He took me straight into the study. You could see half the potteries in Poole from the window, and the sea beyond. He sat me down and he said: 'I know what you're here for, Stanley. You want to marry Stella. But you don't know her,' he said, 'you don't know her.' 'I've been visiting two years, Mr. Glaston,' I said, 'and I think I know my mind.' Then he started talking about her. I never thought to hear a human being talk like that of his own child. He said she was bad—bad in her heart. That she was full of malice. That was why no servants would stay at the Hill. He told me how she'd lead people on, all kind and warm, till they'd told her everything, then she'd hurt them, saying wicked, wicked things, half true, half lies. He told me a lot more besides, and I didn't believe it, not a word. I think I lost my head; I called him a jealous old man who didn't want to lose his housekeeper, a lying, jealous old man who wanted his child to wait on him till he died. I said it was him who was bad, not Stella, and I shouted at him liar, liar. He didn't seem to hear, just shook his head, and I ran out into the hall and called Stella. She'd been in the kitchen, I think, and she came to me and put her arms round me and kissed me.

"We were married a month later, and the old man gave her away. He shook my hand at the wedding and called me a fine man, and I thought what an old hypocrite he was. He gave us money—to me, not her—two thousand pounds. I thought perhaps he was trying to make up for the dreadful things he'd said, and later I wrote to him and said I forgave him. He never answered and I didn't see him often after that.

"For a year or more we were happy enough at Branxome. She was just what I thought she'd be, neat and simple. She liked to go for walks and kiss at the stiles; she liked to be a bit grand sometimes, going to the Dolphin for dinner all dressed up. It meant a lot to me then, I don't mind admitting, going to the right places with Mr. Glaston's daughter. He was Rotary and on the Council and quite a figure in Branxome. She used to tease me about it—in front of other people too, which got me a bit. I remember one time we went to the Dolphin, one of the waiters there was a bloke called Johnnie Raglan. We'd been to school together. Johnnie was a bit of a tear-about and hadn't done anything much since he'd left school except run after girls and get into trouble. Stella knew him, I don't know how, and she waved to him as soon as we'd sat down. Johnnie came over and Stella made him bring another chair and sit with us. The Manager looked daggers, but he didn't dare to do anything because she was Samuel Glaston's daughter. Johnnie stayed there all the meal and Stella talked to him about school and what I was like. Johnnie was pleased as punch and got cheeky, saying I'd been a swat and a good boy and all the rest, and how Johnnie had knocked me about—lies most of it, and she egged him on. I went for her afterwards and said I didn't pay good money at the Dolphin to hear Johnnie Raglan tell a lot of tall stories, and she turned on me fast like a cat. It was her money, she said, and Johnnie was as good as me any day. Then she was sorry and kissed me and I pretended to forgive her."

Sweat was forming on his face; he was talking fast, the words tripping over each other. It was like a man recalling a nightmare, as if the memory were still there, the fear only half gone. He paused and looked sharply at Smiley as if expecting him to speak, but Smiley seemed to be looking past him, his face impassive, its soft contours grown hard.

"Then we went to Carne. I'd just started reading *The Times* and I saw the advert. They wanted a science tutor and I applied. Mr. D'Arcy interviewed me and I got the job. It wasn't till we got to Carne that I knew that what her father had said was true. She hadn't been very keen on Chapel before, but as soon as she got here

she went in for it in a big way. She knew it would look
wrong, that it would hurt me. Branxome's a fine big
church, you see; there was nothing funny about going to
Branxome Tabernacle. But at Carne it was different;
Carne Tabernacle's a little out-of-the-way place with a
tin roof. She wanted to be different, to spite the school
and me, by playing the humble one. I wouldn't have
minded if she'd been sincere, but she wasn't, Mr. Cardew knew that. He got to know Stella, Mr. Cardew did.
I think her father told him; anyway, Mr. Cardew was
up North before, and he knew the family well. For all I
know he wrote to Mr. Glaston, or went and saw him or
something.

"She began there well enough. The townspeople
were all pleased enough to see her—a wife from the
School coming to the Tabernacle, that had never happened before. Then she took to running the appeal for
the refugees—to collecting clothes and all that. Miss
D'Arcy was running it for the school, Mr. D'Arcy's sister, and Stella wanted to beat her at her own game—to
get more from the Chapel people than Miss D'Arcy got
from the School. But I knew what she was doing, and so
did Mr. Cardew, and so did the townspeople in the end.
She listened. Every drop of gossip and dirt, she hoarded
it away. She'd come home of an evening sometimes—
Wednesdays and Fridays she did her Chapel work—and
she'd throw off her coat and laugh till I thought she'd
gone mad.

" 'I've got them! I've got them all,' she'd say. 'I
know all their little secrets and I've got them in the hol-
low of my hand, Stan.' That's what she'd say. And those
that realised grew to be frightened of her. They all gossiped, Heaven knows, but not to profit from it, not like
Stella. Stella was cunning; anything decent, anything
good, she'd drag it down and spoil it. There were a
dozen she'd got the measure of. There was Mulligan the
furniture man; he's got a daughter with a kid near
Leamington. Somehow she found out the girl wasn't
married—they'd sent her to an aunt to have her baby
and begin again up there. She rang up Mulligan once,
something to do with a bill for moving Simon Snow's

furniture, and she said 'Greetings from Leamington Spa, Mr. Mulligan. We need a little co-operation.' She told me that—she came home laughing her head off and told me. But they got her in the end, didn't they? They got their own back!"

Smiley nodded slowly, his eyes now turned fully upon Rode.

"Yes," he said at last, "they got their own back."

"They thought Mad Janie did it, but I didn't. Janie'd as soon have killed her own sister as Stella. They were as close as moon and stars, that's what Stella said. They'd talk together for hours in the evenings when I was out late on Societies or Extra Tuition. Stella cooked food for her, gave her clothes and money. It gave her a feeling of power to help a creature like Janie, and have her fawning round. Not because she was kind, but because she was cruel.

"She'd brought a little dog with her from Branxome, a mongrel. One day a few months ago I came home and found it lying in the garage whimpering, terrified. It was limping and had blood on its back. She'd beaten it. She must have gone mad. I knew she'd beaten it before, but never like that; never. Then something happened—I shouted at her and she laughed and then I hit her. Not hard, but hard enough. In the face. I gave her twenty-four hours to have the dog destroyed or I'd tell the police. She screamed at me—it was her dog and she'd damn' well do what she liked with it—but next day she put on her little black hat and took the dog to the vet. I suppose she told him some tale. She could spin a good tale about anything, Stella could. She kind of stepped into a part and played it right through. Like the tale she told the Hungarians. Miss D'Arcy had some refugees to stay from London once and Stella told them such a tale they ran away and had to be taken back to London. Miss D'Arcy paid for their fares and everything, even had the welfare officer down to see them and try and put things right. I don't think Miss D'Arcy ever knew who'd got at them, but I did—Stella told me. She laughed, always that same laugh: 'There's your fine lady, Stan. Look at her charity now.'

"After the dog, she took to pretending I was violent, cringing away whenever I came near, holding her arm up as though I was going to hit her again. She even made out I was plotting to murder her: she went and told Mr. Cardew I was. She didn't believe it herself; she'd laugh about it sometimes. She said to me: 'It's no good killing me now, Stan; they'll all know who's done it.' But other times she'd whine and stroke me, begging me not to kill her. 'You'll kill me in the long nights!' She'd scream it out—it was the words that got her, the long nights, she liked the sound of them the way an actor does, and she'd build a whole story round them. 'Oh, Stan,' she'd say, 'keep me safe in the long nights.' You know how it is when you never meant to do anything anyway, and someone goes on begging you not to do it? You think you might do it after all, you begin to consider the possibility."

Miss Brimley drew in her breath rather quickly. Smiley stood up and walked over to Rode.

"Why don't we go back to my house for some food?" he said. "We can talk this over quietly. Among friends."

They took a taxi to Bywater Street. Rode sat beside Ailsa Brimley, more relaxed now, and Smiley, opposite him on a drop-seat, watched him and wondered. And it occurred to him that the most important thing about Rode was that he had no friends. Smiley was reminded of Büchner's fairy tale of the child left alone in an empty world who, finding no one to talk to, went to the moon because it smiled at him, but the moon was made of rotten wood. And when the sun and moon and stars had all turned to nothing, he tried to go back to the earth, but it had gone.

Perhaps because Smiley was tired, or perhaps because he was getting a little old, he felt a movement of sudden compassion towards Rode, such as children feel for the poor and parents for their children. Rode had tried so hard—he had used Carne's language, bought the right clothes, and thought as best he could the right thoughts, yet remained hopelessly apart, hopelessly alone.

He lit the gas-fire in the drawing room while Ailsa Brimley went to the delicatessen in the King's Road for soup and eggs. He poured out whisky and soda and gave one to Rode, who drank it in short sips, without speaking.

"I had to tell somebody," he said at last. "I thought you'd be a good person. I didn't want you to print that article, though. Too many knew, you see."

"How many really knew?"

"Only those she'd gone for, I think. I suppose about a dozen townspeople. And Mr. Cardew, of course. She was terribly cunning, you see. She didn't often pass on gossip. She knew to a hair how far she could go. Those who knew were the ones she'd got on the hook. Oh, and D'Arcy, Felix D'Arcy, he knew. She had something special there, something she never told me about. There were nights when she'd put on her shawl and slip out, all excited as if she was going to a party. Quite late sometimes, eleven or twelve. I'd never ask her where she was going because it only bucked her, but sometimes she'd nod at me all cunning and say, 'You don't know, Stan, but D'Arcy does. D'Arcy knows and he can't tell,' and then she'd laugh again and try and look mysterious, and off she'd go."

Smiley was silent for a long time, watching Rode and thinking. Then he asked suddenly: "What was Stella's blood group, do you know?"

"Mine's B. I know that. I was a donor at Branxome. Hers was different."

"How do you know that?"

"She had a test before we were married. She used to suffer from anaemia. I remember hers being different, that's all. Probably A. I can't remember for sure. Why?"

"Where were you registered as a donor?"

"North Poole Transfusion Centre."

"Will they know you there still? Are you still recorded there?"

"I suppose so."

The front door bell rang. It was Ailsa Brimley, back from her shopping.

Ailsa installed herself in the kitchen, while Rode and Smiley sat in the warm comfort of the drawing-room.

"Tell me something else," said Smiley, "about the night of the murder. Why did you leave the writing-case behind? Was it absent-mindedness?"

"No, not really. I was on Chapel duty that night, so Stella and I arrived separately at Fielding's house. She got there before I did and I think Fielding gave the case to her—right at the start of the evening so that it wouldn't get forgotten. He said something about it later that evening. She'd put the case beside her coat in the hall. It was only a little thing about eighteen inches by twelve. I could have sworn she was carrying it as we stood in the hall saying goodbye, but I must have been mistaken. It wasn't till we got to the house that she asked me what I'd done with it."

"*She* asked *you* what you'd done with it?"

"Yes. Then she threw a temper and said I expected her to remember everything. I didn't particularly want to go back, I could have rung Fielding and arranged to collect it first thing next morning, but Stella wouldn't hear of it. She made me go. I didn't like to tell the police all this stuff about us quarrelling, it didn't seem right."

Smiley nodded. "When you got back to Fielding's you rang the bell?"

"Yes. There's the front door, then a glass door inside, a sort of french window to keep out draughts. The front door was still open, and the light was on in the hall. I rang the bell and collected the case from Fielding."

They had finished supper when the telephone rang.

"Rigby here, Mr. Smiley. I've got the laboratory results. They're rather puzzling."

"The exam. paper first: it doesn't tally?"

"No, it doesn't. The boffins here say all the figures and writing were done with the same ballpoint pen. They can't be sure about the diagrams but they say the legend on all the diagrams corresponds to the rest of the script on the sheet."

"All done by the boy after all in fact?"

"Yes. I brought up some other samples of his handwriting for comparison. They match the exam. paper right the way through. Fielding couldn't have tinkered with it."

"Good. And the clothing? Nothing there either?"

"Traces of blood, that's all. No prints on the plastic."

"What was her blood group, by the way?"

"Group A."

Smiley sat down on the edge of the bed. Pressing the receiver to his ear, he began talking quietly. Ten minutes later he was walking slowly downstairs. He had come to the end of the chase, and was already sickened by the kill.

It was nearly an hour before Rigby arrived.

XX

The Dross Of The River

Albert Bridge was as preposterous as ever; bony steel, rising to Wagnerian pinnacles, against the patient London sky; the Thames crawling beneath it with resignation, edging its filth into the wharves of Battersea, then sliding towards the mist down river.

The mist was thick. Smiley watched the driftwood, as it touched it, turning first to white dust, then seeming to lift, dissolve and vanish.

This was how it would end, on a foul morning like this when they dragged the murderer whimpering from his cell and put the hempen rope round his neck. Would Smiley have the courage to recall this two months from now, as the dawn broke outside his window and the clock rang out the time? When they broke a man's neck on the scaffold and put him away like the dross of the river?

He made his way along Beaumont Street towards the King's Road. The milkman chugged past him in his electric van. He would breakfast out this morning, then take a cab to Curzon Street and order the wine for dinner. He would choose something good. Fielding would like that.

Fielding closed his eyes and drank, his left hand held lightly across his chest.

144

"Divine," he said, "divine!" And Ailsa Brimley, opposite him, smiled gently.

"How are you going to spend your retirement, Mr. Fielding," she asked. "Drinking Frankenwein?"

His glass still held before his lips he looked into the candles. The silver was good, better than his own. He wondered why they were only dining three. "In peace," he replied at last. "I have recently made a discovery."

"What's that?"

"That I have been playing to an empty house. But now I'm comforted to think that no one remembers how I forgot my words or missed an entry. So many of us wait patiently for our audience to die. At Carne no one will remember for more than a Half or two what a mess I've made of life. I was too vain to realise that until recently." He put the glass down in front of him and smiled suddenly at Ailsa Brimley. "That is the peace I mean. Not to exist in anyone's mind, but my own; to be a secular monk, safe and forgotten."

Smiley gave him more wine: "Miss Brimley knew your brother Adrian well in the war. We were all in the same department," he said. "She was Adrian's secretary for a while. Weren't you, Brim?"

"It's depressing how the bad live on," Fielding declared. "Rather embarrassing. For the bad, I mean." He gave a little gastronomic sigh. "The moment of truth in a good meal! *Ubergansperiode* between *entremet* and dessert," and they all laughed, and then were silent. Smiley put down his glass, and said:

"The story you told me on Thursday, when I came and saw you . . ."

"Well?" Fielding was irritated.

"About cheating for Tim Perkins . . . how you took the paper from the case and altered it . . ."

"Yes?"

"It isn't true." He might have been talking about the weather. "They've examined it and it isn't true. The writing was all one person's . . . the boy's. If anyone cheated, it must have been the boy."

There was a long silence. Fielding shrugged.

"My dear fellow, you can't expect me to believe that. These people are practically moronic."

"Of course, it doesn't necessarily signify anything. I mean you could be protecting the boy, couldn't you? By lying for him, for his honour so to speak. Is that the explanation?"

"I've told you the truth," he replied shortly. "Make what you want of it."

"I mean, I can see a situation where there might have been collusion, where you were moved by the boy's distress when he brought you the papers; and on the spur of the moment you opened the case and took out his paper and told him what to write."

"Look here," said Fielding hotly, "why don't you keep off this? What's it got to do with you?" And Smiley replied with sudden fervour:

"I'm trying to help, Fielding. I beg you to believe me, I'm trying to help. For Adrian's sake. I don't want there to be . . . more trouble than there need, more pain. I want to get it straight before Rigby comes. They've dropped the charge against Janie. You know that, don't you? They seem to think it's Rode, but they haven't pulled him in. They could have done, but they haven't. They just took more statements from him. So you see, it matters terribly about the writing-case. Every-thing hangs by whether you really saw inside it; and whether Perkins did. Don't you see that? If it was Per-kins who cheated after all, if it was only the boy who opened the case and not you, then they'll want to know the answer to a very important question: *they'll want to know how you knew what was inside it.*"

"What are you trying to say?"

"They're not really moronic, you know. Let's start from the other end for a moment. Suppose it was you who killed Stella Rode, suppose you had a reason, a terribly good reason, and they knew what that reason might be; suppose you went ahead of Rode after giving him the case that night—by bicycle, for instance, like Janie said, riding on the wind. If that were really so, none of those things you saw would have been in the case at all. You could have made it up. And when later the exam. results came out and you realised that Per-kins had cheated, then you guessed he had seen inside the case, had seen that it contained nothing, *nothing but exam. papers.* I mean that would explain why you had to kill the boy." He stopped and glanced towards Field-ing. "And in a way," he added almost reluctantly, "it makes better sense, doesn't it?"

"And what, may I ask, was the reason you speak of?"

"Perhaps she blackmailed you. She certainly knew about your conviction in the war from when she was up North. Her father was a magistrate, wasn't he? I under-stand they've looked up the files. The police, I mean. It was her father who heard the case. She knew you were broke and needed another job and she kept you on a hook. It seems D'Arcy knew too. She told him. She'd nothing to lose; he was in on the story from the start, he'd never allow the papers to get hold of it; she knew that, she knew her man. Did *you* tell D'Arcy as well, Fielding? I think you may have done. When she came to you and told you she knew, jeered and laughed at you, you went to D'Arcy and told him. You asked him what to do. And he said—what would he say?— perhaps he said find out what she wants. But she wanted nothing; not money at least, but something more pleasing, more gratifying to her twisted little mind: she wanted to command and own you. She loved to con-spire, she summoned you to meetings at absurd times and places; in woods, in disused churches, and above all at night. And she wanted nothing from you but your will, she made you listen to her boasts and her mad in-trigues, made you fawn and cringe, then let you run away till the next time." He looked up again. "They might think along those lines, you see. That's why we need to know who saw inside the case. And who cheated in the exam." They were both looking at him, Ailsa in horror, Fielding motionless, impassive.

"If they think that," asked Fielding at last, "how do they suppose I knew Rode would come back for the case that night?"

"Oh, they knew she was expecting you to meet her

that night, after the dinner at your house." Smiley threw this off as if it were a tedious detail, "It was part of the game she liked to play."

"How do they know that?"

"From what Rode says," Smiley continued, "Stella was carrying the case in the hall, actually had it in her hand. When they arrived at North Fields she was without it; she flew into a rage and accused him of forgetting it. She made him go back for it. You see the inference?"

"Oh, clearly," said Fielding, and Smiley heard Ailsa Brimley whisper his name in horror.

"In other words, when Stella devised this trick to gratify her twisted will, you saw it as an opportunity to kill her, putting the blame on a non-existent tramp, or, failing that, on Rode, as a second line of defence. Let us suppose you had been meaning to kill her. You had meant, I expect, to ride out there one night when Rode was teaching late. You had your boots and your cape, even the cable stolen from Rode's room, and you meant to lay a false trail. But what a golden opportunity when Perkins turned up with the hand-case! Stella wanted her meeting—the forgotten hand-case was agreed upon as the means of achieving it. That, I fear, is the way their minds may work. And you see, they *know* it wasn't Rode."

"How do they know? How *can* they know? He's got no alibi." Smiley didn't seem to hear. He was looking towards the window, and the heavy velvet curtains stirring uneasily.

"What's that? What are you looking at?" Fielding asked with sudden urgency, but Smiley did not answer.

"You know, Fielding," he said at last, "we just don't know what people are like, we can never tell; there isn't any truth about human beings, no formula that meets each one of us. And there are some of us— aren't there?—who are nothing, who are so labile that we astound ourselves; we're the chameleons. I read a story once about a poet who bathed himself in cold fountains so that he could recognise his own existence in the contrast. He had to reassure himself, you see, like a child being hateful to its parents. You might say he had to make the sun shine on him so that he could see his shadow and feel alive."

Fielding made an impatient movement with his hand. "How do you know it wasn't Rode?"

"The people who are like that—there really are some, Fielding—do you know their secret? They can't feel anything inside them, no pleasure or pain, no love or hate; they're ashamed and frightened that they can't feel. And their shame, this shame, Fielding, drives them to extravagance and colour; they must make themselves feel that cold water, and without that they're nothing. The world sees them as showmen, fantasists, liars, as sensualists perhaps, not for what they are: the living dead."

"How do you know? How do you know it wasn't Rode?" Fielding cried with anger in his voice, and Smiley replied: "I'll tell you."

"If Rode murdered his wife, he had planned to do so long ago. The plastic cape, the boots, the weapon, the intricate timing, the use of Perkins to carry the case to your house—these are evidence of long premeditation. Of course one could ask: if that's so, why did he bother with Perkins at all—why didn't he keep the case with him all the time? But never mind. Let's see how he does it. He walks home with his wife after dinner, having deliberately forgotten the writing-case. Having left Stella at home, he returns to your house to collect it. It was a risky business, incidentally, leaving that case behind. Quite apart from the fact that one would expect him to have locked it, his wife might have noticed he hadn't got it as they left—or you might have noticed, or Miss Truebody—but luckily no one did. He collects the case, hurries back, kills her, fabricating the clues which mislead the police. He thrusts the cape, boots and gloves into the refugees' parcel, ties it up and prepares to make good his escape. He is alarmed by Mad Janie, perhaps, but reaches the lane and re-enters the house as Stanley Rode. Five minutes later he is with the D'Arcys. From then on for the next forty-eight hours he is under constant supervision. Perhaps you didn't know this, Fielding, but the police found the murder weapon four miles down the road in a ditch. They found it within ten hours of the murder being discovered, long before Rode had a chance to throw it there.

"This is the point, though, Fielding. This is what they can't get over. I suppose it would be possible to make a phony murder weapon. Rode could have taken hairs from Stella's comb, stuck them with human blood to a length of coaxial cable and planted the thing in a ditch *before* he committed the murder. But the only blood he could use was his own—which belongs to a different blood group. The blood on the weapon they found belonged to Stella's blood group. He didn't do it. There's a rather more concrete piece of evidence, to do with the parcel. Rigby had a word with Miss Truebody yesterday. It seems she telephoned Stella Rode on the morning of the day she was murdered. Telephoned at your request, Fielding, to say a boy would be bringing some old clothes up to North Fields on Thursday morning—would she be sure to keep the parcel open till then? . . . What did Stella threaten to do, Fielding? Write an anonymous letter to your next school?"

Then Smiley put his hand on Fielding's arm and said: "Go now, in God's name go now. There's very little time, for Adrian's sake go now," and Ailsa Brimley whispered something he could not hear.

Fielding seemed not to hear. His great head was thrown back, his eyes half closed, his wine glass still held between his thick fingers.

And the front-door bell rang out, like the scream of a woman in an empty house.

Smiley never knew what made the noise, whether it was Fielding's hands on the table as he stood up, or his chair, falling backwards. Perhaps it was not a noise at all, but simply the shock of violent movement when it was least expected; the sight of Fielding, who a moment before had sat lethargic in his chair, springing forward across the room. Then Rigby was holding him, had taken Fielding's right arm and done something to it so that Fielding cried out in pain and fear, swinging round to face them under the compulsion of Rigby's grip. Then Rigby was saying the words, and Fielding's terrified gaze fell upon Smiley.

"Stop him, stop him, Smiley, for God's sake! They'll hang me." And he shouted the last two words again and again: "Hang me, hang me," until the detectives came in from the street, and shoved him without ceremony into a waiting car.

Smiley watched the car go. It didn't hurry, just picked its way down the wet street and disappeared. He remained there long after it had gone, looking towards the end of the road, so that passers-by stared oddly at him, or tried to follow his gaze. But there was nothing to see. Only the half-lit street, and the shadows moving along it.

ABOUT THE AUTHOR

JOHN LE CARRÉ is the pseudonym of David Cornwell.
Born in 1931, he attended the universities of Berne and
Oxford, taught at Eton and later entered the British
Foreign Service. He has been described in *The New
York Times* as belonging to the select company of
such spy and detective story writers as Arthur Conan
Doyle, Dashiell Hammett, Raymond Chandler, and Ross
Macdonald. His first two novels were *Call for the Dead*
(1961) and *A Murder of Quality* (1962). His third
novel, *The Spy Who Came in from the Cold* (1963),
was greeted with great enthusiasm and secured his world-
wide reputation. Mr. le Carré is also the author of *The
Naive and Sentimental Lover, The Looking Glass War,
A Small Town in Germany, Tinker, Tailor, Soldier, Spy,
The Honourable Schoolboy, Smiley's People* and *The
Little Drummer Girl*.

JOHN LE CARRÉ

"The premier spy novelist of his time. Perhaps of all time," is what *Time* magazine recently called him.

Others echo the praise. But it took John le Carré many years to reach this position. He began his writing career while in the British Foreign Service. Unable to use his real name (David Cornwell) because the Foreign Office forbids its staff to publish under their own names, he adopted the name le Carré (French for "the square") which he claims to have seen printed on a London shop window.

As he states, "When I first began writing, Ian Fleming was riding high and the picture of the spy was that of a character who could have affairs with women, drive a fast car, who used gadgetry and gimmickry to escape." What le Carré has brought back is the realistic spy story.

Call for the Dead and *A Murder of Quality* were his first novels. It was his third novel *The Spy Who Came in from the Cold* which broke through to bestsellerdom. It features the antihero Alec Leamas, a cold war spy, out to rescue friends from Berlin. In *The Looking Glass War* our hero learns of the double-dealing needed to survive in the intelligence game. A change of pace, *A Naive and Sentimental Lover* follows an unhappy but successful businessman beguiled by a glamorous, wayward couple. *Tinker, Tailor, Soldier, Spy* followed. George Smiley (a minor character in *The Spy Who Came in from the Cold*) is the hero. Head of a British Intelligence department he must ferret out the "mole" who has wasted some of the department's best agents. Le Carré's bestseller *The Honourable Schoolboy* deals with Smiley's attempts to use one of his friends as a pawn to flush out a pair of mysterious Chinese brothers. *Smiley's People* chronicled Smiley's final confrontation with his greatest enemy, Karla. His latest #1 bestseller, *The Little Drummer Girl* will be published in paperback by Bantam in April 1984.

Le Carré, who has elevated the spy novel to its highest point, is a demon on research. For *The Honourable Schoolboy* he made five trips to Southeast Asia. Pinned down by automatic weapons fire in Cambodia, he dived under a car and coolly noted his impressions on file cards.